PUFFIN BOOKS

JUMANJI

'It's so weird,' Alan said. 'I mean, where does the drumming come from?' He picked up the box and read about the game. '"Jumanji. A game for those who seek to find a way to leave their world behind. The first to get to the end of the path and yell 'Jumanji' wins."'

Sarah picked up the dice and studied them disdainfully. 'I quit playing board games five years ago.'

She dropped the dice on to the board. One rolled a 4, the other a 2. Without warning, one of the tokens moved to the sixth square: it seemed like magic. Sarah and Alan gaped at the board, then at each other.

Jumanji

A novelization by Todd Strasser
Based on a screenplay by Jonathan Hensleigh
and Greg Taylor & Jim Strain
Based on a screen story by Greg Taylor &
Jim Strain and Chris Van Allsburg
Based on the book by Chris Van Allsburg

PUFFIN BOOKS

PUFFIN BOOKS

Published by the Penguin Group
Penguin Books Ltd, 27 Wrights Lane, London w8 5tz, England
Penguin Books USA Inc., 375 Hudson Street, New York, New York 10014, USA
Penguin Books Australia Ltd, Ringwood, Victoria, Australia
Penguin Books Canada Ltd, 10 Alcorn Avenue, Toronto, Ontario, Canada m4v 3b2
Penguin Books (NZ) Ltd, 182–190 Wairau Road, Auckland 10, New Zealand

Penguin Books Ltd, Registered Offices: Harmondsworth, Middlesex, England

First published by Puffin Books as a film tie-in 1996
3 5 7 9 10 8 6 4 2

Copyright © TriStar Pictures Inc., 1995
All rights reserved

The moral right of the author has been asserted

Filmset by Datix International Limited, Bungay, Suffolk
Set in 12/14pt Monophoto Palatino
Printed in England by Clays Ltd, St Ives plc

PROLOGUE

Deep in the New England forest the howling wind bent the trees back, rattling their limbs and snapping off great branches as if they were twigs. Blown by the wind, the harsh rain ripped through the dark air at an angle and the forest creatures cowered in their lairs.

Crack! Lightning tore a bright gash through the stormy night sky and the thunder rumbled ominously. At the side of a narrow muddy road a pair of horses, hitched to a small wooden wagon, whinnied in fear and stamped the ground with their hoofs.

A stone's throw away, in the dark shadows beneath the shaking trees, two young brothers worked with bent backs in a deep hole, digging furiously. Their trousers were muddy and their faces streaked with dirt and rainwater. Their long-handled spades scraped and clanked as they threw clod after clod of earth out of the hole.

1

'Deep enough!' the older boy yelled, his voice filled with fear and urgency.

He and his younger brother flung their spades to one side as they scrambled out of the hole. Together they started towards the wagon, but fear prevented the younger boy from coming closer. The older boy reached into the back of the wagon and started to slide a heavy, locked iron box out of it.

The box was heavy, and the older boy couldn't manage it alone. 'Come on!' he yelled to the younger boy. 'We're almost rid of it!'

Pale with fear, the younger boy came forward to help his brother drag the box into the woods. At the edge of the hole, grunting with effort, they threw the box in.

'*Help!*' Suddenly the younger boy lost his footing on the slippery ground and tumbled into the hole, landing on top of the box.

Brummm-tum-tum. Brummm-tum-tum . . . A mysterious – but all too familiar – drumming sound arose out of the hole.

'*It's after me!*' the younger boy screamed in terror, and he pawed frantically at the earth at the side of the hole, desperately trying to escape. But his feet kept slipping back, as if whatever was inside the box was trying to keep him down in that grave-like cavity.

'Grab on!' his older brother shouted, leaning over the edge and reaching down. The younger boy stretched up, caught hold of his brother's slippery hands, and felt himself being pulled out.

Brummm-tum-tum! Brummm-tum-tum! As if angered, the drumming in the box grew louder.

'*Run! Run!*' the younger boy cried hysterically and started to dash away.

'No!' His older brother grabbed him by the shirt and pulled him back. 'We have to finish this! Come on! Help me bury it!'

The older boy took his spade and began to shovel the loose earth back into the hole. Reluctantly at first, his younger brother joined in. Soon the drumming sound began to fade as the box disappeared under the dark, wet soil.

Boom! Thunder crashed and lightning crackled above them as the exhausted boys dragged their spades back to the wagon and climbed in. The older boy cracked a whip, and the horses were all too eager to go.

With his wet hair plastered to his head and his teeth chattering, the younger boy looked back at the spot where they'd buried the mysterious box.

'What if someone digs it up?' he asked with a shiver.

'May God have mercy on his soul,' his brother replied. He pulled on the reins, and they rode away through the dark, stormy night, never to return.

BRANTFORD, NEW HAMPSHIRE, 1969

It was a warm September afternoon. A slight, thin, twelve-year-old boy was pedalling his new three-speed bike along the tree-lined main street of town, past the low brick and clapboard buildings. As he passed the baker's, the florist's and a draper's shop, he waved to the shopkeepers and pedestrians, all of whom waved back. After all, the boy's name was Alan Parrish, and his family was the richest in town.

Alan kept on pedalling along. He was a friendly boy and was not at all affected by his family's wealth. Even as he rode through the town square, passing the tall, bronze statue of his great-great-grandfather, Angus Parrish, a Civil War hero, his mind was on other things.

'Prepare to die, Parrish!' The sudden sound of Billy Jessup's voice sent a chill of fear through Alan. Twisting around, he saw Billy and a group of boys with long hair racing

towards him on their bikes. Alan instantly leant on the pedals of his bike and his legs started to go round as if his life depended on it.

'Hey, Parrish!' Billy yelled with a cruel laugh as he and his friends sped after him. 'What's the rush?'

Alan continued to pedal furiously. It was easy enough to laugh when it was five against one – as long as you weren't the *one*! He turned on to a street that was lined with tall old oak-trees. Alan kept riding as hard as he could but, glancing over his shoulder, he could see that the boys behind were catching him up . . . with Billy Jessup in the lead.

'Come on, Parrish!' Billy yelled gleefully. 'Let's get it over with!'

Ahead was a car park and, just beyond that, a tall brick building. A large sign on the side of the building read:

PARRISH SHOES – FOUR GENERATIONS OF QUALITY

Alan raced through the gates leading to the car park, then he jumped off his bike and ran into the building beyond. Behind him, Billy and the other boys skidded to a halt.

'Go ahead, Parrish!' Billy yelled. 'Run to Daddy! Just remember: we'll be waiting!'

Standing in the cool shadows just inside the factory doors, Alan paused to catch his breath. He'd escaped ... *for now*. He composed himself and set off up the stairs. The strong, sharp smell of fresh leather greeted him.

He reached the top of the stairs. A cavernous factory, as big as a football pitch, stretched out in front of him, filled with the echoing din of machinery and workmen's voices. Alan started to walk down a long aisle that was lined with men cutting patterns from leather and sewing shoe parts together.

Thunk-a-thunk-a-thunk! He paused beside the loud, rumbling, sole-stamping machine that chopped shoe soles out of the leather.

Carl Bentley, a twenty-year-old man with dark skin, looked up and smiled. 'Hey, my man, Alan!' he said.

Relieved to hear a friendly voice, Alan turned towards him. 'Hi, Carl.'

'Let me show you something,' Carl said, pausing from his work on the assembly line to reach into a drawer. 'I've been working on this for almost a year now. I've got an appointment to show it to your father this afternoon.'

Carl pulled a shoe out of the drawer. Alan

had never seen anything like it before: it was some kind of plimsoll, made of canvas and white leather above a rubber sole.

'What do you think?' Carl asked eagerly, handing the plimsoll to Alan.

'Uh, what is it?' Alan asked uncertainly.

Carl's jaw dropped. 'What is it? It's a proto-type of the *future*! In a couple of years, there's gonna be a pair of these in every cup board in America. This shoe is gonna be the height of fashion and . . .'

Alan didn't hear the rest. Still worried about Billy Jessup and his friends, he'd walked over to a window and was looking down at the car park.

'Something wrong?' Carl asked, joining him.

'Uh, no, nothing.' Alan never liked to dis-cuss his problems with anyone.

The familiar smell of pipe smoke drifted towards him. Alan turned and saw his father walking along the assembly line. Sam Parrish was in his early forties. He had thin-ning brown hair, he smoked a pipe and wore a jacket and tie. He owned the shoe factory, and he never seemed to go any-where without two or three men in attendance.

'What are you doing here?' Mr Parrish

asked his son sternly. 'I've told you before, this factory isn't a playground.'

Alan put Carl's prototype plimsoll down on an idle conveyor-belt. 'I, er, wanted to see if you could give me a ride home.'

Mr Parrish narrowed his eyes. 'Billy Jessup again?' he guessed.

Alan wasn't surprised his father had worked out the real reason he'd come to the factory. He started to regret that he'd gone there seeking refuge.

'I've told you this before, son,' Mr Parrish said. 'You're going to have to deal with that bully sooner or later.'

Alan wanted to explain that it wasn't Billy alone, but four of his friends as well. But he was already feeling humiliated enough in front of Carl and the men who always followed his father around.

'If you're afraid of something, you've got to face it,' Mr Parrish said, giving Alan a pat on the shoulder. 'Now, get along, son.'

It was no use trying to explain. Alan shrugged and started to walk back up the aisle towards the stairs. Suddenly a horn began to blare behind him. Alan turned and saw men scurrying around, waving their arms and yelling. Something had gone wrong with the sole-stamping machine. Alan could feel the vibrations running through the floor as the machine began to shudder and smoke. Bolts were flying and blades snapped.

Then, all at once, it went dead. Silence descended on the factory floor as the workers stopped what they were doing and stared at the machine. Alan watched his father pull open a hatch on the side of the machine and yank out a gnarled handful of leather and canvas strips.

It was Carl's prototype! Alan realized with a start. Meanwhile, his father's face was red with anger.

'Who did this?' he demanded.

Carl Bentley swallowed nervously. From the end of the aisle, Alan wanted to call out that it wasn't Carl's fault, that *he'd* accidentally put the prototype on the conveyor-belt. But he couldn't bring himself to suffer his father's cross-examination again.

Instead, he hurried down the stairs and back out into the sunny car park. His bike was still there, and Billy and his pals seemed to have gone. Breathing a sigh of relief, Alan climbed on his bike and started to ride away.

But no sooner was he out of the car park than Billy and his friends appeared from behind the trees and blocked his path.

'Going somewhere?' Billy asked with a nasty grin.

Alan shot a quick look around, but it was no use. He was surrounded.

2

Alan felt himself start to tremble but managed to control himself. Billy Jessup took a step towards him.

'Just because you're a Parrish doesn't mean you can hang around with my girlfriend,' Billy said.

Alan couldn't believe it. 'You mean Sarah? But we've always been friends.'

'Not any more,' Billy said, making his hands into fists and moving towards Alan.

A second later, all five boys were on him, kicking and punching. Alan fought back, but he didn't really stand a chance.

It was over in less than three minutes. Laughing and jeering, Billy and his friends left, taking Alan's new bike with them. Alan struggled to his feet. His head was throbbing and his lip was split. Blood from his nose and mouth had dripped all over his shirt – but it didn't matter because the shirt was torn anyway.

Jerks, he thought as he started to trudge home along the tree-lined road. But there was no way that he was going to let his father see him in that condition.

Brummm-tum-tum. Brummm-tum-tum ... He hadn't gone far when a strange drumming sound reached his ears. Alan looked around but saw nothing that could have caused the sound. He shook his head and set off along the road again.

Brummm-tum-tum. Brummm-tum-tum ... There it was again. Alan put his fingers in his ears, wondering if perhaps Billy had given him concussion.

Brummm-tum-tum!   *Brummm-tum-tum!* The drumming kept growing louder. Alan had the feeling that it was calling him. Curious and puzzled, he started to follow the sound.

The drumming led him to a construction site. A sign said: 'Future Executive Offices of Parrish Shoes'. But all Alan could see was a big yellow bulldozer digging huge gaping holes in the ground.

Brummm-tum-tum!   *Brummm-tum-tum!* Alan followed the drumming sound. All around, construction workers wearing hard hats were going about their work as if they couldn't hear a thing. Were they deaf?

13

A hooter blared and the workers dropped their tools. Alan noticed a silver snack van parked at the edge of the construction site. It must be time for a coffee break. Everyone left the site and made for the van. All except Alan, that is, who was still following the source of the drumming.

Finally, he found the hole it was coming from. Alan jumped down into it and stood there, surrounded by walls made of earth.

Brummm-tum-tum! *Brummm-tum-tum!* The noise was coming from one particular place in the earth wall. Alan picked up a spade and scraped away some of the earth. A rusty, reddish-brown handle appeared. Alan took hold of it and pulled.

Thump! The box landed at the bottom of the hole. The drumming stopped and everything became quiet. Alan stared down at it. He'd never seen anything like it before. An ancient lock kept the box closed, but it was completely rusted.

Clang! Alan hit it with the spade and it fell off at once. Hopefully imagining that it was filled with ancient treasures, Alan bent down, and raised the lid of the box. *What the . . .?* It was filled with sand. Nothing but sand.

Disappointed, Alan started to climb back out of the hole.

Brummm-tum-tum. Brummm-tum-tum ...
The drumming started again. Alan felt
goose-pimples rise on his skin. He quickly
turned back to the box and plunged his
hands into the sand. They met something hard, and he tugged out a wooden
box.

Alan stared down at it in wonder. It
looked like a box for cutlery or a games
compendium: the fold-up kind with brass
hinges and a clasp. And it was decorated
with carvings of jungle animals, landscapes,
and a great white hunter complete with
pith helmet. Above all that, in elaborate
and fanciful type, was the word
JUMANJI.

Alan had never heard of it, and he won-
dered if it was some kind of game. He shook
the box and things inside rattled. Intensely
curious, he undid the clasp and opened it
ever so slightly ... just for a peep.

A flash of glorious, rich colour seeped out.
Alan was stunned.

'So I think we'd better start laying the foun-
dation here.'

'Ferro-concrete or cinder blocks?'

Alan could hear the voices of men return-
ing to the site. He snapped the box shut,
tucked it under his arm and scampered out

of the hole. Whatever this thing was, he was going to take it home and give it a closer and more thorough inspection.

3

Various chores, and a long explanation to his mother about what had happened to his nose and his clothes, kept Alan from opening the Jumanji box until later that evening. Now he was sitting alone at the long wooden table in the dining room. Hanging on the walls were portraits of the famous men and women of the Parrish family who'd sat at that table decades before. His great-great-grandfather's Civil War sabre lay on the mantelpiece above the fireplace.

Slowly and carefully, he opened the box. It unfolded into a game board. From the edges of the board, four different paths curled and wound their way towards a strange, cloudy, glass-like circle in the centre. In a small side-drawer he found tokens and dice.

Alan picked up one of the tokens. It was carved like a miniature African totem.

'Hard work, determination and a cheerful outlook . . .' His father's words came drifting towards him from the large, marble-lined hall. Alan quickly snapped the board closed and hid it under his chair.

'These attributes have exemplified the Brantford spirit since our forefathers first settled this town,' his father was saying.

Alan relaxed a little as he realized that his father was not delivering this latest lecture to *him*. Instead, he appeared to be practising it for an audience he would face later that night.

'Despite the granite of our soil, and the harshness of our native climate, we have . . . Darn it, what?'

'Wasn't it prospered?' Alan heard his mother offer. 'Or was it persisted?'

'I can't remember,' his father said. 'I had the whole thing memorized this morning, but I've forgotten.'

'Well, darling,' Alan heard his mother say, 'if you can face the town council, you can certainly face your son.'

Alan stiffened. *Oh-oh.* His father *did* have something to say to him.

A second later, his father strode into the dining room wearing a dinner jacket. His mother followed, wearing a red and white evening gown. She was the first to speak.

'Alan, darling, I told your father what you

told me this afternoon,' she said. 'That it wasn't just Billy Jessup.'

'If I'd known there were five boys,' Mr Parrish said awkwardly, 'I wouldn't have lectured you.'

Wishing to spare his father any further embarrassment, Alan told him it was OK. He hoped his parents would now go, but they lingered. His mother kept nodding at his father, as if there was something else she wanted him to say.

'Well, er, I want you to know that I'm proud of you for facing them, even though you were outnumbered,' Mr Parrish continued, fumbling for something in his pocket. 'And, since you took it like a man, I want you to see this.'

He handed Alan a booklet with, on its cover, a photograph of some ivy-clad red-brick buildings. It looked like a college campus.

'Your mother and I have decided that you're ready to go to the Cliffside Academy for Boys,' his father announced. 'You proved it today.'

'Congratulations, sweetheart,' his mother chimed in.

Alan felt numb, as if he'd just gone into shock. The Cliffside Academy for Boys was a boarding school in Connecticut.

19

What was happening was obvious to him at once: his parents were getting rid of him.

'You don't want me living here any more.' The words sort of spilled from his lips.

'Oh, Alan, how could you possibly *think* such a thing?' his mother gasped.

'You're ashamed of me for getting beaten up all the time,' Alan said.

'Absolutely not,' his father insisted. 'I just told you how proud I am of you.'

Rubbish, Alan thought.

'It had always been the plan that you'd go to Cliffside when you were ready,' his father added. 'We Parrish men have been going there since the seventeen hundreds.'

Feeling miserable, Alan pulled his glasses out of his pocket and studied the booklet more closely – and immediately wished he hadn't.

'Look at this,' he said, pointing to one of the pictures. '"Parrish Hall."'

'It's the main dormitory,' his father explained.

'Great.' Alan rolled his eyes. 'I get beaten up here because my name is Parrish. I can't wait to see what they'll do when I'm living in a building named after me.'

His father looked shocked. 'It was named after my father.'

All the frustration that had been building

up since the fight suddenly spilled out of Alan. 'Good,' he snapped bitterly. 'Why don't *you* go and live in it?'

His father stiffened, biting back a more angry response. 'I *did* live in it. And I wouldn't be who I am today if it weren't for my years there.'

'So?' Alan asked angrily. At that moment he hated being a Parrish; all it meant to him was being picked on and beaten up.

His father's jaw clenched. 'Don't get smart with me, son.'

'I'm not,' Alan shot back. 'Maybe I don't want to be who you are! Maybe I don't even want to be a Parrish!'

His father's face turned red with anger. Mrs Parrish put a hand on her husband's shoulder to calm him.

'Believe me, son,' Mr Parrish growled through clenched teeth. 'You won't be, not until you start acting like one!'

'So I guess I'm not ready to go to Cliffside,' Alan said, drawing the conclusion that he'd hoped they would all reach.

'We're taking you there next Sunday,' his father replied in an icy voice. 'And I don't want to hear another word about it.'

'You won't!' Alan almost yelled. 'I'm never going to talk to you again!'

Father and son glared at each other. At that moment it seemed to Alan that this was all his father's fault. Alan hated being a Parrish, he hated living in this house and being next in line to inherit that stupid shoe company. He hated *all* of it!

Without saying another word, Mr Parrish turned and signalled for his wife to follow him out of the room. Alan sat silently and watched them go. As soon as his father had pulled the door shut behind him, Alan picked up the booklet for Cliffside and tore it into little pieces.

Forget it! He wasn't going there. Ever! Alan jumped up from his seat and made his way upstairs. He was leaving, getting out, going somewhere no one had ever even *heard* the name Parrish.

4

A little while later, Alan was to be seen carrying a small suitcase towards the front door. Inside were some clothes, a few sandwiches, cakes and biscuits, and that Jumanji game. He was on the point of pulling the front door open and storming out when *Ding! Dong!* the doorbell rang.

Now what? Alan quickly hid the suitcase under a table in the hall and pulled the door open. Outside stood Sarah Whittle, a pretty, blonde thirteen-year-old, who, unfortunately, was the source of a great deal of Alan's misery. Behind her was Alan's racing bike.

'Oh, it's you.' Alan turned away and picked up the suitcase.

'Going somewhere?' Sarah asked.

'Yeah, I'm . . .' He stopped. Maybe he shouldn't tell her. 'I was just going over to Billy's to get my bike.' He stepped past her.

'With a suitcase?' Sarah asked suspiciously.

Alan didn't answer. Instead, he started to strap the suitcase to the rack behind the bike's seat. The truth was, he'd had a mad crush on Sarah since the age of ten. But the only thing it had got him was a black eye and a swollen lip.

'I told Billy that, if he didn't give you your bike back, I wouldn't go to the movies with him this weekend,' Sarah said.

'Great, thanks a lot.' Alan's words were heaped with jealous sarcasm.

'Hey, I just wanted him to stop picking on you,' Sarah explained. 'I was trying to do you a favour.'

'Save it for your boyfriend.' Alan snapped the kick-stand up and started to push the bike away.

'Billy's *not* my boyfriend,' Sarah replied. Then she added, 'But at least he's my age.'

That was the big problem. Alan was a year younger than Sarah.

'Yeah – but mentally I could be his grand-father,' Alan said, continuing down the front path with his bike. 'And I'm *only* ten months younger than you.'

'But you're so *immature*,' Sarah said behind him.

'Fine,' Alan shot back over his shoulder. 'Have a great life with Billy.'

Brummm-tum-tum. Brummm-tum-tum ...
Alan froze. The drumming sound had
started inside his suitcase.

After a moment it stopped.

'What was that?' Sarah asked.

'Nothing.' Alan started pushing the bike
again.

Brummm-tum-tum. Brummm-tum-tum ... It
began again. Sarah came closer and stared at
the suitcase.

'What's *in* there?' she asked, mystified.

Alan looked out at the road. He really
wanted to get going, but he really wanted to
show her the game, too. Finally the game,
and Sarah, won.

'You gotta see this,' Alan said, turning the
bike around and heading back towards the
house. 'It's really cool.'

Moments later they were going through
the glass french windows between the living
room and the dining room. Alan put the suitcase on the floor and opened it.

Brummm-tum-tum! *Brummm-tum-tum!*
The drumming grew louder as he took the
game board out and opened it. Sarah
watched, fascinated.

'It's so weird,' Alan said. 'I mean, where
does the drumming come from?' He picked
up the box and read about the game.

' "Jumanji. A game for those who seek to find a way to leave their world behind. The first to get to the end of the path and yell 'Jumanji' wins." '

Sarah picked up the dice and studied them disdainfully. 'I quit playing board games five years ago.'

She dropped the dice on to the board. One rolled a 4, the other a 2. Without warning, one of the tokens moved to the sixth square: it seemed like magic. Sarah and Alan gaped at the board, then at each other.

'It must be magnetized or something,' Alan said, picking up the dice.

But Sarah was scarcely listening. Her eyes went wide as she pointed to the glass-like lens in the middle of the board. Words were appearing in the glass . . . as if it was some kind of crystal ball.

' "At night they fly, you'd better run," ' Alan read. ' "These winged things are not much fun." '

The letters faded away. Suddenly Alan heard flapping and fluttering sounds coming from the fireplace.

'What's that?' Sarah asked apprehensively.

'I don't know, maybe a bird or something,' Alan said. But deep inside he knew it wasn't

a bird. Something weird was going on ...
weird and scary.

'Put it away,' Sarah said, meaning the
board.

'Yeah, you're right.' Without thinking,
Alan let the dice fall on the board. They
rolled a 2 and a 3. Now another token was
moving to the fifth square.

'Uh – oh!' Alan gasped as more words
began to appear in the crystal. '"In the
jungle you must wait, until the dice read five
or eight." What's *that* mean?'

Suddenly Sarah shrieked, '*Alan, what's happening to you?*'

Alan didn't have a clue what she was talking about. 'What do you mean? Nothing's
happening...' Then he looked down at
his body: his legs and arms were melting!
And he was being sucked into the game
board!

'Wha ... *Ahhhhhhhhhh!*' A scream of terror
ripped from Alan's throat as his whole body
turned into a liquid mass and was sucked
into the board. The next thing he knew, he
was looking up at Sarah and the living room
and the chandelier hanging from the ceiling
as if through a fish-eye lens.

'Alan? *Alan!?*' Sarah was screaming down
at the board. As Alan watched helplessly

from inside, she suddenly looked away. Another scream was torn from her throat as hundreds of big black bats burst from the fireplace, swooping and diving at her.

In a flash she was up and gone. Alan was left behind, somewhere inside the game.

5

THE PRESENT

Eight-year-old Peter Shepherd was not happy. Ever since his parents had been killed in that car crash in the Canadian Rockies, his life had been a jumbled, mixed-up mess. At the moment, Peter and his twelve-year-old sister, Judy, found themselves standing on the front lawn of a big, old, creepy-looking house in Brantford, New Hampshire.

They were with their Aunt Nora, a grand sort of lady in her thirties who seemed to have taken over their lives now that their parents were gone. The problem was, Aunt Nora had never been married and had never had children of her own. She knew as much about looking after children as an Eskimo knows about surfing.

'Judy! Peter!' Aunt Nora waved to them from the front door. 'Come and look at this.'

Judy gave Peter a sullen look and they started towards the front door of the house. Aunt Nora was looking for a big house to buy so that she could turn it into something called a 'bed and breakfast'. When Judy asked what that was, Nora had said it was like a cross between an inn and a private home. Peter still wasn't at all sure what she meant by that.

He and his sister entered the house and looked around. They were standing in a room which had a marble floor and a chandelier, made of a zillion pieces of glass, hanging from the ceiling. The house smelled old and musty. Peter stepped into the living room. All the furniture was covered with old, yellowed bed-sheets and there was dust everywhere. Peter couldn't imagine anyone wanting to stay there.

Aunt Nora was walking around with another lady, who was older than she was, and who had long, bright red fingernails.

'I'm going to put a reception area right here,' Aunt Nora told the lady. 'And a bar over there in the parlour.'

'That sounds lovely,' the red-nail lady said. Peter had noticed that, no matter what Aunt Nora said, the red-nail lady said it sounded lovely.

Now the red-nail lady looked down at Peter. 'So, what do *you* think, young man? Is this place big enough for you?'

Peter turned and walked out of the room. Behind him he could hear Aunt Nora tell the red-nail lady that he hadn't said a word since the accident. The red-nail lady pretended to be sad and said it was awful. That got Peter's sister Judy started.

'It's OK,' she told the red-nail lady. 'We barely knew our parents. They were always away skiing or gambling or sailing. We didn't even know whether they loved us, but when their boat started to sink they wrote us a really beautiful goodbye note which someone found in a champagne bottle.'

It was all a lie, but that was the only way Judy seemed to be able to deal with her parents' death. Aunt Nora took the red-nail lady aside and whispered something.

After a while the red-nail lady left and Aunt Nora made them help her unpack the car and bring in the boxes and suitcases. Then she took them out for pizza and ice-cream. When they got back, it was time to go to bed.

At bedtime Peter went into his new bedroom and Judy went into hers. Aunt Nora came and said some stupid stuff about her not being his mother, but how she was going to try her best anyway. It was the same as what she said almost every night. Then she left, and Peter lay there and waited until he was fairly certain she wouldn't come back. Then he pulled open the drawer of his bedside table and took out a photograph of his mum and dad.

Brummm-tum-tum. Brummm-tum-tum ... The faint sound of jungle drums seemed to be coming from the ceiling.

Peter glanced up at the ceiling, then he looked back down at the photograph.

The doorknob began to turn. Peter had just enough time to slip the photograph back into the drawer before the door opened and Judy came in, wearing pyjamas with pink flowers on them.

'Move over,' she said.

Peter slid across and made room for her in the bed and Judy got in.

'Did you hear something before?' she asked.

Peter stared up at the ceiling and thought of the drums, but he decided not to mention it.

'Me neither,' Judy said with a shrug, but Peter knew she was lying.

He turned and faced her. 'I miss Mum and Dad,' he whispered. 'Do you?'

'No,' Judy whispered back.

Peter studied his sister's face for a

moment. 'If you don't quit lying, you're gonna get sent to a shrink.'

'Where do you think they're going to send *you* if you don't start talking?' his sister asked.

Peter didn't know the answer to that, and he didn't want to talk about it. He turned over on his side and closed his eyes.

Brummm-tum-tum. Brummm-tum-tum ... The faint sound of drums began their beating again.

Peter's eyes popped open. He glanced at his sister, who was looking back at him, wide-eyed. She snuggled closer and he pulled the blanket up under his chin. It would be a long time before either of them fell asleep that night.

6

The next day, at their new school, Peter and Judy learned all about the history of the house they'd moved into. At breaktime the other children told them how twelve-year-old Alan Parrish had vanished from the house twenty-six years earlier and had never been seen again. Some kids said it was a kidnapping. Others claimed that Alan's father had chopped him up into little pieces and had hidden them all over the house.

Then Judy told the other kids how her parents had been abducted by Maoist guerrillas in New Guinea, where they'd gone to research some strange new rainforest viruses. Peter stood near by and said nothing.

Then a big fat boy announced that Judy was lying. He said his mother was the red-nail lady who had sold the Parrish house to their aunt, and that their real parents were dead.

And that's when Peter went a little crazy

and attacked the big fat boy. But he just laughed and held Peter at arm's distance where he could swing his fists all he liked and still not land a punch.

So Peter bit him on the arm as hard as he could and the big fat boy screamed and ran away. Then the other children all made a circle round Peter and called him an animal until Judy fought her way through them and dragged Peter away.

'I can't believe I have to talk to the principal after just *one* day of school,' Aunt Nora groaned that night in the kitchen where they were eating dinner. 'What am I supposed to do with you? This is *not* my department.'

'You'd better punish us,' Judy suggested.

'What's the punishment for lying?' Aunt Nora asked, nervously twisting a napkin round her fingers. 'Or for biting someone?'

'You should probably ground us,' Judy replied.

'OK, you're both grounded,' Aunt Nora said. Then she sighed. 'Now . . . let's just try to relax and finish our dinner. Let's talk about something else.'

A long silence followed. Then Judy cleared her throat.

'Well, we found out why no one else ever bought this house,' she said. Then she told Aunt Nora how, twenty-six years before, a boy named Alan Parrish had been chopped into little pieces by his father and scattered round the house.

Aunt Nora's eyes started to grow wide, then slowly narrowed. 'That's *it!*' she snapped. 'I'm sick and tired of your lies, young lady. You're grounded!'

'You already did that one,' Judy informed her.

Aunt Nora gave her a helpless look, as if she didn't know any other good punishments.

'Send me to my room,' Judy recommended.

Aunt Nora nodded wearily and Judy stood up.

'Just for your information,' Peter's sister said, 'that wasn't a lie.'

Then she left the room. Peter and Aunt Nora finished dinner in silence.

The next morning, Aunt Nora had to leave early. She gave Peter and Judy breakfast, then made them sit on the stairs while she issued her instructions: 'The school bus should be here any minute. There's a snack for you in the fridge for when you get home. If I get held up at the permit office, I'll call.'

Brummm-tum-tum. Brummm-tum-tum . . . That was when the drums started their gentle banging upstairs again. Peter and Judy glanced up, then they looked at their aunt, who just kept on talking as if she hadn't heard a thing. They looked at each other, then up towards the noise again.

'Hello?' Aunt Nora put her hands on her hips and looked annoyed. 'Are either of you listening to me?'

'Huh?' Judy frowned.

The drumming stopped.

Aunt Nora sighed. 'Maybe I should wait here with you until the bus comes. Did your parents put you on the bus?'

Peter started to nod, but Judy quickly shook her head and said, 'No.'

'Are you sure?' Aunt Nora asked.

'Positive,' said Judy. 'You can go. We'll be fine.'

'All right, be good.' Aunt Nora turned and went out through the front door.

Judy quickly got up and closed the door behind her. Then she turned to Peter. 'You *do* hear it,' she said.

'Hear what?' Peter asked innocently.

Brummm-tum-tum. Brummm-tum-tum . . .

The drumming started again. Clearly, it was coming from above them. In a flash they were both racing up the stairs to the first floor.

But when they reached the first floor, the drumming was still coming from above. Judy looked nervously at the spiral staircase leading to the attic, then she started up it. Peter followed.

Once they got to the attic, however, the drumming stopped again. Peter and Judy looked around, bewildered. The attic was filled with old furniture, paintings, sports equipment and toys. There was even a piano, but no sign of any drums.

'Where was it coming from?' Judy asked in a low voice.

Peter shook his head. He didn't know. They split up and started to search.

Brummm-tum-tum!   *Brummm-tum-tum!*
Without any warning, the drumming started again, immediately behind Judy.

'*Ahhh!*' Judy let out a scream and wheeled around.

Meanwhile Peter ran over and began to dig through a pile of old toys, jigsaw puzzles and hockey sticks. At the bottom of the pile was a wooden box with the word JUMANJI carved on it.

Brummm-tum-tum!   *Brummm-tum-tum!*
The drumming was louder than ever and it was definitely coming from the box.

Peter reached down in order to pick up the box but, just as he was about to touch it, the drumming stopped. He frowned at Judy, who nodded encouragement. Peter picked up the box and set it down, gently, on top of an old dresser. Then he carefully opened its clasp and unfolded the game.

'Wow!' Judy let out a deep breath as she studied the game board. Curiously, two tokens had already been placed on it. Peter tried to move them, but they wouldn't budge.

'Weird,' he said. 'They're stuck.'

From the drawer at the side he took out two more tokens and the dice. Meanwhile Judy was reading the instructions printed on the outside.

Shuump! Suddenly the two loose tokens in Peter's hands were sucked on to their first squares on the board. Peter and his sister sat back in shock.

'It's gotta be microchips or something,' Judy guessed.

Peter handed her the dice. 'You go first.'

Judy stared reluctantly at the dice in her hand. 'Well, OK.' She let the dice fall on the board.

Brummm-tum-tum! Brummm-tum-tum! The drumming started again, and Judy's piece moved by itself. She and Peter exchanged amazed glances. Then some words began to appear in the crystal in the middle of the board.

'"A tiny bite can make you itch,"' Judy read. '"Make you sneeze, make you twitch"'

A loud, buzzing sound reached their ears. Judy and Peter spun around just in time to see three mosquitoes the size of sparrows heading straight for them.

7

Peter had never seen such huge mosquitoes. Judy quickly picked up an old tennis racket and swung it.

Whack! She hit the lead mosquito. *Crash!* It was sent smashing through an attic window. The other two mosquitoes banked sharply and followed it outside.

Peter and Judy stared at each other in amazement, then they looked down at the board. Peter picked up the dice, but Judy grabbed his hand.

'Don't!' she cried.

It was too late. Peter let the dice fall and rolled two 1s.

Brummm-tum-tum! Brummm-tum-tum! The drumming started again. (Peter hadn't even noticed that it had stopped.) New words began to appear in the crystal: 'This will not be an easy mission. Monkeys slow the expedition.'

Crash! Clang! Thwack! A cacophony of

things breaking loudly started to come from downstairs. Judy jumped up and raced towards the attic stairs. Peter picked up the dice and followed her.

As they ran down the stairs towards the kitchen, they could hear the sounds of plates being smashed, accompanied by weird, screeching cries. Judy came to a halt behind the kitchen door, then she slowly pushed it open.

Inside, a dozen large brown monkeys were demolishing the kitchen. Perched on one of the worktops, two monkeys were throwing porcelain cups at a third monkey, who was swinging a ladle like a baseball bat and smashing them to fragments. Other monkeys were busy hurling all the food out of the refrigerator, while still others were throwing knives around!

Judy hastily closed the kitchen door. She and Peter stared at each other, spellbound. Then Peter gazed fearfully at the dice in his hand. Without doubt, they were the cause of all the trouble.

'Listen, Peter,' Judy muttered in a low, urgent voice. 'We'd better get back upstairs and take another look at that game.'

In a flash they were racing back up the stairs. Gasping for breath, they burst into the attic once more. Judy picked up the board and quickly read through the instructions: 'OK, you roll the dice and move.'

'We know that,' Peter said.

'Doubles gets another turn,' his sister read. 'The first player to reach the end and yell "Jumanji" wins.'

'That's it?' Peter asked.

'No, there's this too.' Judy read: '"Adventurers, beware: do not begin unless you intend to finish. The exciting consequences of the game will vanish only when a player has reached Jumanji and called out its name."'

Creak! Wham! Downstairs, the front door opened, then slammed shut again. Judy and Peter raced to an attic window, just in time to see the monkeys fan out across the lawn below and disperse in a dozen different directions.

'We have to stop them!' Peter dashed back to the game and began to fold it up.

'No, wait!' Judy stopped him. 'The instructions say the only way we can make it all go away is if we finish the game. We'd better do it, or Aunt Nora's gonna have a fit!'

Peter glanced nervously at the game board. So far, they'd been attacked by giant mosquitoes and had unleashed a bunch of maniac monkeys, who'd already destroyed the kitchen and were now running around in Brantford doing who knew what!

Judy could see that her brother was reluctant to start playing again. 'Listen,' she said, 'we'll get through it quickly. Just keep rolling the dice. I mean, there's no *skill* involved.'

Peter hesitated, then he unfolded the board and held the dice out to his sister.

'No.' She shook her head. 'Snake's eyes is doubles. You get another turn.'

Peter rolled a 3 and a 5. As his token moved across the board without him touching it, words appeared in the crystal: 'His fangs are sharp, he likes your taste. Your party better move post haste.'

'Post haste?' Judy scowled. She'd never heard of that.

The crashing sound of piano keys being hit by a fist made them jump. Peter and his sister spun around and squinted into a dark corner of the attic where an old piano stood. A huge lion emerged from the shadows and fixed them with its steady eyes.

Peter and Judy started to back away. Peter's mouth was open, but his throat was so tight with fear that no sound could escape.

GRRROAARRRR! The lion let out a terrifying roar. Peter and Judy bolted to the door and flew down the spiral stairs.

Thwaammp! Somehow the lion had leapt the entire staircase and was now cutting them off on the first floor.

'Ahhhhhh!' Peter and his sister let out a scream in unison and raced along the first-floor hall in the opposite direction. Then they both skidded to a halt. Standing in front of them was a wild man! He had long, stringy, brown hair and a bushy beard. His clothes were stitched together from animal hides, and on his head he wore a primitive-looking hat made from a tortoise shell. His clothes glistened with raindrops, as if he'd just stepped out of a tropical rainforest.

He had a crazy look in his eyes and was holding a crude-looking knife in his hand.

Caught between the wild man and the lion, Peter and Judy looked both ways along the hall: at one end was the ferocious lion; at the other was a wild man with a knife.

And they were trapped in the middle!

8

GRRROAARRRR! The lion leapt to the attack!

Given the choice between that huge, deadly beast and the wild man, the children made straight for the man. To their surprise, he let them run right past him. The next thing Peter knew, Judy had pushed him into a linen cupboard and had pulled the door closed behind her, leaving it open just enough for them both to peep through.

Meanwhile the lion was launching itself at the wild man!

At the last possible moment, the wild man leapt up, grabbed the hall chandelier and hung from it in mid-air.

The lion missed him and landed hard on the carpet edge. Its momentum sent it sliding all the way into Aunt Nora's bedroom.

The wild man let go of the chandelier and dropped down to the hall floor. *Wham!* He kicked Aunt Nora's door shut.

GRRROAARRRR! Inside the bedroom, the lion roared its anger. Then *Blam!* It charged the bedroom door and smashed into it. Five long claws ripped through the thin wood of the door, but the lock held.

In the linen cupboard, Peter and Judy held their breath as the wild man turned away from the door and touched the hallway wall as if he was studying it. Then he walked along the hall towards them. Terrified, Peter and Judy backed deeper into the linen cupboard and pulled the door completely shut.

But the doorknob turned and the door flew open. The wild man was standing there, looking in at them.

'*Ahhhhhh!*' Peter and his sister screamed again. But the wild man seemed to take no notice of them.

Wham! He slammed the linen cupboard door again. Inside the dark cupboard, Peter and Judy heard his footsteps start to move away. Once again Judy pushed the door open just far enough to see. The wild man was standing in the middle of the hall with a stunned look on his face.

A second later he whipped around and bounded towards another door. He tugged at the knob, but the door must have been locked.

Bam! He kicked the door down and went in.

As curious now as they were frightened, Peter and Judy slowly sidled out of the linen cupboard and crept to the doorway the wild man had just gone through. Inside was a boy's bedroom; it had posters of base-ball players on the walls and plastic models on the shelves. The wild man was standing next to an old, dust-covered racing bike, running his fingers along its dusty cross-bar.

They watched as he opened a cupboard door and gazed at the boy's clothing that was hanging inside. Then he turned to a chest of drawers and picked up a curled, yel-lowed photograph. From a pouch at his waist he took out a battered pair of glasses that were much too small to fit on his head. Holding the glasses up to his eyes, he stud-ied the photograph for a long time.

Then he turned slowly towards Peter and Judy, who were still standing in the doorway.

'Did someone roll a five or an eight?' he asked.

Peter nodded.

'Yes!' the wild man cried out and bounded towards him. Peter turned to run but, before he could make a move, the wild man had scooped him up in his arms and was starting to dance round the room, shouting with joy. But then he stopped.

Thunk! He dropped Peter and ran out of the room.

Peter got to his feet and gave Judy a puzzled look. A second later, they were running out of the room and down the stairs to the ground floor, where the wild man was dashing from room to room.

'Mum! Dad' he shouted. 'Where are you? It's me, Alan! I'm home!'

Peter and Judy shot an amazed look at each other. Could this really be the boy whose father had chopped him into little pieces?

'Excuse me,' Judy said. 'You're not Alan Parrish, are you?'

Alan Parrish, now thirty-eight years old, spun around. 'Who are you?'

'I'm Judy and he's Peter.' Judy said. 'We live here now.'

Alan stared at them with a strange smile on his lips as if he didn't understand.

'This house has been empty for years.' Judy explained. 'Everyone thought you were dead.'

Alan just kept on staring at them. Finally

his lips began to move. 'So . . . where are my parents?'

Judy glanced nervously at Peter. 'We don't know.'

The smile disappeared from Alan's face. He turned and ran through the hall and out through the front door.

Peter and Judy followed him. Alan crossed the lawn and walked out into the street, looking all around.

Screeech! A shiny, brand-new police car that had been coming down the street jammed on its brakes to avoid hitting the wild-looking man. At the last second Alan leapt into the air and landed on the car's bonnet.

The car rolled to a stop and the policeman inside jumped out, at the same time shouting at Alan, 'Get down off my car!'

Alan got down.

'Step up on the sidewalk,' the policeman ordered. Instead of following Alan on to the pavement, however, the policeman stared at the bonnet of his car and, using the sleeve of his shirt, rubbed at the spot where Alan had stood until it was shining again.

Meanwhile Alan was gazing into the police car with a fascinated look on his face.

'Excuse me,' the policeman said.

'What year is it?' Alan asked.

'It's brand new,' the policeman replied, referring to his car.

'No,' Alan said. 'I mean, what *year* is it?'

The policeman stared at Alan as if he was crazy.

'It's 1995,' Judy said, coming up behind them.

The policeman rolled his eyes. 'You got some ID?' he asked Alan.

But Alan was mumbling to himself: 'Ninety-five minus sixty-nine ... twenty-six years?'

'Let me guess,' the policeman said very drily, staring at the stitched-together animal skins Alan was wearing. 'You left your wallet in your other pants. OK, maybe you can tell me this. You from around here?'

'Yes,' said Alan. 'But I've been in Jumanji.'

'Huh?' the policeman scowled.

'It's in Indonesia.' Judy quickly said. 'He was in the Peace Corps.'

Meanwhile Alan was studying the nametag on the policeman's uniform. 'Carl Bentley?'

Officer Bentley turned to Judy. 'Is this man related to you?'

'Yes, sir.' Judy lied as to the manner born. 'He's our uncle.'

Peter noticed that two of the monkeys from the game were now trying to crawl into Officer Bentley's car. Officer Bentley didn't see them – but Alan must have, because he let out a loud roar that sounded just like a lion. In a flash the monkeys had disappeared behind the car.

Officer Bentley frowned and turned to Judy again. 'Is he OK upstairs?' he asked.

'He suffered a head injury a few months ago,' Judy explained hurriedly. 'You know how, when you're on a train, you're not supposed to stick anything out of the window?'

K-BOOM! A sudden explosion made everyone jump. Peter spun around and stared at Officer Bentley's car. Smoke was rising through a blackened hole in the roof. The monkeys had got inside and one of them must have fired Officer Bentley's riot gun! The other one turned the key in the ignition!

Screeech! The police car took off, leaving skid marks all along the street. Peter couldn't see anyone driving, but he could hear wild monkey laughter coming from inside.

'Stop!' Officer Bentley shouted and started to run down the street after his new patrol car. No sooner had he left than Alan set off at a brisk pace in the opposite direction.

'Wait!' Judy gasped. 'Where are you going?'

'To find my parents,' Alan replied.

'But what about the game?' Judy asked. 'It says we have to finish.'

'Go ahead and finish,' the wild man yelled back over his shoulder, without pausing for a moment.

9

Instead of finishing the game, Judy and Peter followed him. It appeared that Alan knew the way into town. Soon he was walking along Main Street, past a string of pawn-shops, off-licences and boarded-up build-ings. Alan strode along, looking this way and that, with a shocked expression on his face as if he couldn't believe what had become of his town. Not knowing what to say, Peter and Judy followed silently.

Alan walked right through the town and made his way towards a big brick building with broken windows. On the side of the building, a large rusty sign, faded and pep-pered with bullet holes, read:

PARRISH SHOES — FOUR GENERATIONS OF
QUALITY

Judy and Peter went through the gates and into the factory behind Alan. Inside, the build-ing was full of ancient, rusted machines.

Birds chirped and flew around in the rafters above and water dripped from the ceiling, leaving puddles on the floor.

They watched Alan bend down and pick up an old shoebox, cradling it in his hands like a broken doll. 'Where is everybody?' he asked in a bewildered voice. 'There used to be hundreds of workers. My dad made shoes here ... the best shoes in New England.'

Suddenly he noticed something upstairs – the silhouette of a man smoking a pipe in the doorway. Alan raced up the stairs as fast as he could. Peter and Judy hurried behind him and watched as he pushed open the door.

Inside, an old man was reclining in a chair, smoking a pipe. Some blankets were lying in the middle of the garbage on the floor, and a pot of water was steaming over a small portable gas-stove. It occurred to Judy and Peter that the old man must be a tramp who lived here.

The old man looked startled by the sudden intrusion.

Alan looked crushed. 'I'm sorry,' he muttered to the old man. 'I thought you were someone else.'

They watched as Alan turned to leave, but then he stopped and looked back at the old man. 'Do you know what happened to the shoe factory?'

'It folded,' the old man replied, relighting his pipe and puffing on it. 'Like everything else in this town.'

'What about the Parrish family?' Alan asked.

'After their kid disappeared, they put everything they had into trying to find him,' the old man replied. 'After a while Sam stopped coming to work. He just quit caring.'

Alan winced.

'Some of us tried to keep the place going,' the old man said, 'but I guess we just didn't have the Parrish touch.'

Alan gave a slight shiver. It *was* a little chilly, especially for someone who'd been in a jungle for the past twenty-six years.

The old man pointed at a pile of clothes lying on the floor. 'You'd better take something,' he said.

Alan picked out a pair of olive-coloured, flared trousers. 'Are the Parrishes still around?' he asked as he pulled the trousers on.

'Oh, yeah,' the old man said with an ironic smile. 'They're over on Adams Street.'

Peter and Judy followed Alan out of the factory and along several tree-lined streets, to a cemetery. Once there, Alan slowed down. His shoulders drooped and his head hung low as he began to read the grave-stones. They watched as he dropped to his knees, then took off his home-made tortoise-shell hat and placed it on a gravestone.

'I bet that's his parents',' Judy whispered to Peter as they stood near by, watching.

Then Alan lifted his hands to his face and pressed them there, muttering something about wishing his family didn't exist.

'Our parents are dead, too,' Judy said. 'They were in the Middle East, negotiating peace, when –'

Before she could continue, Peter poked her in the ribs. He'd had enough of her wild stories.

'Our dad was in advertising,' he said.

Judy stared at him in wonder. This was the first time Peter had spoken to another human being, except her, since the accident.

Alan stared at Peter, then he got to his feet and set off once more through the graveyard.

'There he goes again,' said Judy. 'Come on.'

They had to run to catch up with him.

'Listen,' Judy said as she jogged alongside Alan, 'I know you're upset and all, but I was hoping you could help my brother and me finish the game.'

Alan shook his head. 'Sorry.'

'You could be a little grateful,' Judy said. 'Without us, you'd still be stuck in there.'

'I'm forever in your debt for getting me out,' Alan replied, not very sincerely. 'But it wouldn't make a whole lot of sense if the first thing I did was go and get stuck in there again, would it? I'm not interested in playing that game. I have too much catching up to do.'

'But you don't understand,' Judy said. 'There's a lion in my aunt's bedroom!'

'Call a zoo,' Alan replied shortly. 'I'm out of the lion business.'

10

Because they couldn't think of anything else to do, they followed Alan out of the grave-yard. The sound of a siren got Peter's atten-tion. He looked up and saw an ambulance racing along Main Street.

Screeech! Tyres squealed as the ambulance swerved to avoid a car that was weaving er-ratically in the opposite direction. The vehi-cles clipped each other and skidded to a halt not far from where Alan, Peter and Judy were standing.

A paramedic in a white shirt and dark trousers jumped out of the ambulance and ran across to the other car. He yanked open the door and pulled out the driver. Peter's jaw dropped. It was the red-nail lady! She was staggering about and seemed barely con-scious. Her skin was yellow and jaundiced, and her face glistened with sweat.

'Here's another one!' the paramedic shouted to his partner, who was dragging a stretcher out of the back of the ambulance.

'That's over fifty!' his partner yelled back. 'What in the world's going on?'

Alan stepped closer and studied the red-nail lady's face. Then he cocked his head as if listening to something.

'Hear that?' he said to the children.

'Hear what?' Judy replied. Peter couldn't hear anything either, but it didn't matter. Alan could hear something – and it made him turn pale with fright.

'Quick! Move it!' he yelled, shoving them towards the red-nail lady's car. They all piled into the front. Alan slid into the driver's seat and slammed the door shut.

'Think!' he urged them. 'What came out of the game before?'

'There was the lion,' Judy said. 'A bunch of monkeys and –'

'That!' Peter cried, pointing through the windscreen at a giant mosquito that had just landed on the car's bonnet. The mosquito peered through the window and poked at it with its needle-like proboscis. Inside the car, the children held their breath in sheer fright.

'Don't worry,' Alan reassured them. 'It can't get us in here.'

As if the mosquito had heard him, it flew up off the bonnet of the car and disappeared.

Ripppp! Something slashed through the car's canvas roof. Looking up, Peter saw the mosquito's proboscis stretching down, trying to reach them. He and Judy shrank as far away from it as they could.

Unable to reach them, the mosquito withdrew again.

'We're safe,' Alan said with a sigh of relief. 'Those things'll make you ill if they bite you, but if we go home and stay inside we'll be OK.'

Crack! They all looked up, startled. In a furious attempt to reach them, the mosquito had smashed into the windscreen, cracking it.

'How are we going to get home?' Judy asked worriedly.

Peter watched as Alan studied the car's dashboard. The keys were still in the ignition.

'Do either of you know how to drive?' Alan asked.

Judy and Peter shook their heads.

'I didn't think you looked old enough.' Alan shrugged. 'OK, no problem,' he added, reaching for the keys. 'My dad let me back the car down the driveway once, and he used to let me sit in his lap and steer all the time.'

He turned the key and the car started. 'OK, here we go!'

The car's engine revved up as Alan pressed on the accelerator, but they didn't move an inch. The lines in Alan's forehead deepened as he studied the dashboard again and started pulling buttons.

Peter heard a whirring sound as the canvas roof started to lift and fold back.

'Alan!' Judy cried. 'The top!'

Looking up, they saw the sky appear where the top had been. And growing larger and larger in the sky was the mosquito, dive-bombing straight at them!

Peter reached over and tugged at the thing he'd once seen his father pull on to make their car go.

Screeech! The car took off down the street, weaving and zigzagging as Alan tried to steer it.

Crunch! Bang! Clang! Crack! In quick succession they destroyed a phone box, a STOP road-sign, fifty feet of picket fence and a post box, before finally coming to a halt in the front garden of the Parrish house.

Alan released a pent-up breath, grinned and dusted his hands together. 'Piece of cake,' he said cheerfully.

Meanwhile Judy and Peter practically had

to prise their hands off the dashboard and door handles. They'd even left finger marks, they'd been clinging on so hard! Peter had been on some pretty scary roller-coasters, but nothing to compare with this.

Alan pushed open the car door and headed for the house. Judy and Peter followed, wondering what would happen next. It didn't take long for them to find out. When they got inside, Alan had disappeared!

11

They found him in the attic, standing in front of a mirror and holding an old, wrinkled shirt up against himself. From an already open trunk he pulled out a pair of trousers.

'Alan?' Judy came up behind him, holding the Jumanji game. 'When are you going to help us play?'

At the sight of the game, Alan shrank back, his eyes wide with fear. 'Keep that thing away from me!'

'But we have to finish before Aunt Nora comes home,' Judy said pleadingly.

'Good, then I can inform her that she's the *ex*-owner of this house.' Alan picked up a bundle of clothes and set off past them towards the attic stairs. 'You realize that, with my parents gone, this place is mine now.'

They followed him down to the first storey, where he went into the bathroom and dropped the clothes on the floor. 'How's the hot water these days? Did anyone replace that old boiler?'

Bang! He closed the door on Judy and Peter.

Judy knocked. 'You have to help us finish the game. What do you think those monkeys are going to do to the ecosystem around here? Hello?'

It was no use. The hissing sound of a running shower was Alan's answer. Peter gave his sister a quizzical look, as if to ask what they could do now. Judy answered by sitting down in the hall outside the bathroom door. They'd wait.

When the bathroom door finally opened, it was a new man who stepped out. He was wearing an old shirt and trousers and his wet hair was much shorter, with a somewhat ragged look. His face was covered with nicks and cuts that had been covered with scraps of toilet paper. Both the children winced.

'Hey, what do you want?' Alan asked defensively. 'I never shaved before.'

They followed him down to the kitchen, which looked as if a bomb had gone off in it. Tables and chairs were overturned, dishes and bowls had been smashed on the floor, and every surface was covered with food of one sort or another.

Alan found a bowl under the counter

and, much to Peter's and Judy's disgust, started to fill it with whatever half-decent morsels of food he could find.

'How about Peter and I play the game, and you just sort of watch?' Judy asked.

'No, thanks.' Alan shook his head. 'I've seen all I want. Besides, I don't plan further ahead than my next meal. I learned that the hard way.' He held up an almost whole doughnut. 'Bingo!'

'Well, if you aren't going to help us, what *are* you going to do?' Judy asked.

Alan stopped and blinked, as if he hadn't considered that before. 'I guess I'll just pick up where I left off. I wonder if Mrs Neder-meyer still teaches sixth grade?'

He leant across to the refrigerator door and pulled it open.

'*Ah!*' A gasp of fright left his lips as a shivering monkey jumped out, screeched abuse at him and then ran out of the room.

Peter watched as Alan took a moment to gather himself again. It gave Peter an idea. 'Come on, Judy,' he said, getting up. 'Alan's not going to help us. He's afraid.'

'What?' Alan spun around. 'What did you say?'

'I said you're afraid,' Peter replied. 'But it's OK to be afraid.'

'It's OK to be afraid,' Alan repeated in a mocking tone. 'I am *not* afraid.'

'Prove it,' Peter said.

Alan stared at him for a moment. 'I don't have to prove anything to you.'

Peter ignored him and turned to his sister. 'Let's set the game up in the living room.'

They made to leave the kitchen.

'Hey, listen,' Alan said from behind them. 'You don't know what you're getting yourselves into.'

'Whatever it is, we'll handle it ourselves,' Peter replied. 'We don't need you. Come on, Judy.'

'You think monkeys and mosquitoes and lions are bad?' Alan called after them. 'That's kids' stuff. I've seen things that would give you nightmares for the rest of your life!'

Peter kept walking, pretending he wasn't impressed.

'I've seen things you can't even imagine!' Alan said again. 'Snakes as long as a school bus, spiders the size of bulldogs, things that hunt in the jungle at night, things you can't even see. You can just hear them running – and eating. You think it's "OK to be afraid". You don't know what fear is. Believe me, you won't last five minutes without me.'

That's when Peter halted and spun around. 'So you're going to help us play?'

Alan must have realized that he'd backed himself into a corner. 'All right! All right! I'll play!'

Peter breathed an immense sigh of relief. He noticed Judy staring at him in wonder.

'That was very cool,' she whispered in awe.

'Reverse psychology,' Peter replied. 'Dad used to pull it on me all the time.'

12

While Peter was setting the board up on the coffee table in the living room, Alan went around the room pulling the shades down.

'Everybody ready?' Judy asked, holding up the dice.

'Ready!' Peter said eagerly.

'Ready,' Alan groaned reluctantly.

'OK, here I go!' Judy tossed the dice. Everyone waited with bated breath.

Judy's piece on the board didn't move. Nothing happened.

'I'll try again.' Judy picked up the dice and rolled them.

Still nothing happened.

Peter and his sister looked across to Alan.

'It's not working,' Judy said.

Alan rubbed his chin and stared at the board. 'No, right, of course not! It's not your turn!'

'It has to be,' Judy said. 'I rolled first. Then

Peter went twice because he got doubles. Now it's my turn again.'

'No, look!' Alan pointed at the board. Four tokens stood on various squares. 'Those two are yours. This one's mine. There's one more.'

'Whose is it?' Judy asked.

Alan stared at the board again as realization dawned on him. 'You're playing the game I started in 1969!'

'So whose turn is it?' Judy asked.

'The person I was playing with,' Alan replied.

Peter and Judy waited for him to explain further, but Alan just gazed away into the distance.

'Well,' Judy said impatiently at last. 'Who was it?'

'Sarah Whittle,' Alan replied.

'Who?'

Without saying another word, Alan stood up and left the room.

Judy looked at Peter. 'Here we go again,' she said with a moan.

Alan left the house and set off along the road. Once again Peter and Judy smiled at each other.

A little while later, they were following Alan through a gate and up a path towards a house. Trees hung over the path and the grass was long and unruly and full of weeds. The house itself looked run-down. Shutters hung by a single hinge and the paint everywhere was peeling.

'This place gives me the creeps,' Peter whispered to his sister as he looked around.

They stopped by a sign on the porch. In hand-painted purple letters it said:

MADAM SERENA, PSYCHIC READINGS
BY APPOINTMENT ONLY

Alan's shoulders sagged with disappointment. 'I knew she wouldn't still be here.'

'Let's at least ask,' Judy said. 'Maybe Madam Serena will know where Sarah went.'

While Judy was knocking at the door, Alan looked around on the porch. 'We used to play right here on this porch. It seemed a lot bigger in those days.'

A moment later, a muffled female voice could be heard on the other side of the door. 'Yes?'

'Can you help us?' Judy asked.

'Do you have an appointment?' the woman asked.

'No, we're just trying to find someone.'

'Madam Serena can't see you right now,' the woman said.

'Maybe *you* can help us,' Alan chimed in.

The door opened slowly and Peter saw a pretty lady with dishevelled blonde hair and puffy eyes standing there. It looked as if she'd been asleep and they had woken her.

'We're looking for someone who used to live here,' Alan explained.

The woman frowned and studied him closely. 'I've lived here all my life.'

'Then you must know Sarah Whittle!' Judy exclaimed.

'Why do you want Sarah Whittle?' the woman asked suspiciously.

For the last few seconds Alan had been transfixed, silently staring at the woman. Now he said, 'Sarah?'

'I . . . I don't go by that name any more,' the woman stammered, staring back at him.

'Sarah Whittle?' Alan said once more, as if he could hardly believe it.

'What do you want?' the woman asked, narrowing her eyes at him.

'When you were thirteen, you played a game with a kid down the street,' Alan said, stepping closer. 'A game with drums.'

Sarah went white. 'How do you know *that*?'

72

'Because I was there,' Alan said.

She stared up at him, round-eyed. 'Alan?'

'Yes.' Alan nodded.

Thunk! Sarah Whittle went as stiff as a board and fell over backwards in a dead faint.

13

They revived her and, after a great deal of persuasion, convinced her that she should come back with them to the Parrish house. There, sitting on a couch in the living room, she insisted on making a phone call.

'Sounds like I got his answering machine,' she muttered to herself while the others tried not to listen. Peter heard a faint beep on the other end of the phone, then Sarah started to talk into it. 'Dr Boorstein, it's Sarah Whittle calling. I might need to have my dosage checked. You know the event we've been talking about for the past two decades? The one that didn't really happen? Well, I seem to be having another episode involving that little boy who didn't really disappear. I'm sitting in his living room, drinking lemonade. I'd be very interested in your interpretation. Please call me at your next opportunity.'

She hung up. 'He'll call back at ten minutes to the hour.'

Alan and the children exchanged glances. 'OK. Now, while we are waiting...' He drew the Jumanji board out from under the coffee table.

'*Ahhhhh!*' Sarah jumped to her feet. 'Get that thing *away* from me!'

'You have to help us finish the game, Sarah,' Judy said.

'No, I don't!' Sarah cried. 'I've spent over two thousand hours in therapy convincing myself that that thing doesn't exist! I made it all up about you turning into smoke and disappearing into the game, because whatever *really* happened was just too awful!'

Alan nodded. 'It was awful, but it was also real.'

'No!' Sarah took a step back, still shaking her head. 'Your father murdered you and chopped you into little pieces and hid you in the walls.'

Alan looked startled. '*My* father did that?'

Sarah nodded.

Alan smiled. 'Sarah, you knew my father. He could barely *hug* me, let alone chop me into little pieces.'

'Well, it's *always* the repressed types,' Sarah muttered.

'Listen,' Alan said in a calming voice. 'Twenty-six years ago we started something, and now we're all going to finish it. And guess what?'

Sarah gave him an extremely anxious look as he took her hand . . . and dropped the dice in it.

'It's *your* turn,' Alan said.

'I won't play.' Sarah kept shaking her head.

'You *will* play,' Alan insisted.

Sarah narrowed her eyes and hissed, 'Just try and make me.'

They glared at each other.

Finally, Alan sat down. 'All right,' he said in a disgusted tone, holding out his hand. 'Just give me the dice – and get out!'

Sarah let go of the dice. Instead of catching them, Alan let them fall on the game board!

'How could you do that!' Sarah screeched. 'That's not fair!'

'Sorry.' Alan shrugged. 'Law of the jungle.'

Brummm-tum-tum! Brummm-tum-tum! The drumming started. Everyone stared at the board. Sarah's token slid itself forward.

Meanwhile Sarah was staring daggers at Alan. 'When I think of all the energy I've put into visualizing you as a radiant spirit,' she grumbled.

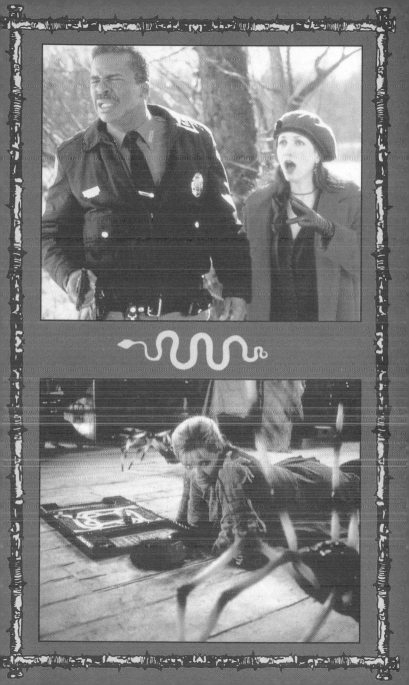

Words began to float up into the crystal, but Sarah refused to look at them.

'Go on,' Judy urged her. 'Read it.'

But Sarah's eyes were locked on Alan. 'Twenty-two years of Dr Boorstein down the drain. All I can say is . . . I'm incredibly lucky I had health insurance.'

'*Read it!*' Alan snarled.

Sarah took a deep breath and swallowed. ' "They grow much faster than bamboo. Take care or they'll come after you." '

Bits of plaster started to drop on the game board. Everyone looked up at the ceiling, where the green tendril of a vine was forcing its way through a crack in the plaster.

'Don't let this be happening!' Sarah moaned.

Peter looked round the room: small vines were starting to push out from behind pictures, from between the cushions of the sofa, and out of the electrical sockets. Everyone backed into the centre of the room and huddled there.

'Stay away from the walls,' Alan cautioned them.

The green tendrils began to bloom with purple flowers the size of sunflowers.

'Wow, they're beautiful.' Sarah reached

out to touch one, but Alan grabbed her hand and pulled her back.

'Don't touch them!' he warned. 'They shoot poison barbs. And don't go anywhere near the big yellow ones.'

Judy looked around. 'What big yellow ones?'

Suddenly Peter felt something curl round his ankle and tighten. 'Help!' he cried, but it was too late. The vine jerked him off his feet and started to pull him under the rug.

'Get him!' Alan shouted.

They raced after him, but the vine was pulling too fast. Peter twisted around just in time to see a giant green pod appear at the far end of the room. The thing must be four feet wide! Suddenly it opened, revealing yellow petals and pointed, shark-like teeth.

It was a yellow one! And it was pulling him towards its gaping vegetable jaws.

'Noooooooooo!' Peter screamed in total terror.

At the last second Alan dived forward and took hold of Peter's free ankle. Sarah and Judy each grabbed one of his hands. Then all three began to pull. They got into a tug-of-war with the vine, using Peter as the rope!

Grunting and straining every muscle, they pulled as hard as they could. Peter thought that his arms and legs were going to pop right out of their sockets.

And still the vine was pulling him closer to the huge yellow flower's teeth!

14

Frozen with terror and stretched about as far as he could be, Peter's eyes stayed locked on Alan as the older man looked around desperately for something to help them. Then he made a sudden lunge for the old Civil War sabre hanging above the stone fireplace.

But, in doing so, he had to let go of Peter!

'Heeeellllllppppp!' Peter screamed as the vine dragged him ever closer to the yellow pod. His feet were now only inches away!

Whack! Alan slammed the sabre down, slicing the vine in two. Like a tug-of-war team whose rope accidentally breaks, everyone rocketed backwards and landed in a heap on the floor. Peter opened his eyes, to see a cloud of feathery white things floating in the air above him.

'Seeds,' Alan said, getting to his feet. 'Whatever you do, *don't* open any windows. You wouldn't believe how fast these things grow.'

He ran to the pair of french windows that separated the living room from the dining room and slammed them shut. New tendrils from the vine were snaking up on the other side of the glass, but they were unable to get through.

Meanwhile Sarah had got to her feet and was quietly easing her way towards the front hall as if to escape. Just as she turned to run, Alan dashed across the room and grabbed her.

'Get your hands off me!' Sarah tried to twist out of his grasp.

'The game's not over yet,' Alan grunted through clenched teeth as he struggled with her.

'It is for *me!*' Sarah kept on fighting him. 'Let me go!'

But at last Alan managed to drag Sarah back to the living room. Peter and Judy followed them to the game board and watched as Alan forced Sarah to sit down.

'We'll finish the game right here,' Alan announced.

'This is so abusive,' Sarah complained with a pout.

Judy picked up the dice and handed them to Alan. 'It's your turn.'

Sarah groaned again and shook her head.

'The last time I played this game, it ruined my life.'

'It ruined *your* life?' Alan's eyes went wide and manic. 'What about *mine*? "In the jungle you must wait, until the dice read five or eight." Remember? But they didn't read five or eight for twenty-six years *because somebody stopped playing*!'

Sarah winced sheepishly. 'I . . . I was just a kid. I couldn't handle it.' She glanced at Peter and Judy, as if asking for their support.

'It's OK,' Judy said. 'We're scared, too. But if we finish the game, it's all supposed to go away.'

'How do you know?' Sarah asked nervously. 'How do you know it won't all happen again? How do *I* know I won't get stuck in the jungle next?'

Alan turned his level gaze on her. 'Because, unlike some people, Sarah, I won't abandon my friends.'

'Neither will I,' said Judy.

Everyone looked at Peter, and he put out his hand. Judy placed hers on top of it, and Alan put his hand on top of hers, as if making a gesture of unity.

They all turned to Sarah.

'Well?' Alan asked with a slightly teasing look.

Sarah sighed and rolled her eyes, then, reluctantly, she put her hand on top of the others. 'I knew this was going to be a bad day.'

'Relax,' Alan said, shaking the dice in his hand. 'All we have to do is roll with the punches and keep our heads. Everything's going to be fine.'

Wearing a smile brimming with reassurance, Alan let the dice drop. His token moved and new words began to float up into the crystal lens.

'"A hunter from the darkest wild makes you . . . feel just like a . . ."' Alan turned pale and didn't finish the sentence.

'Child?' Judy guessed.

Alan shrank down into a frightened child-like crouch. His eyes darted around. 'Van Pelt,' he whimpered.

Blam! A shotgun blast shattered the french windows of the living room. A cloud of feathery vine seeds wafted towards them in the air.

'*Get down!*' Alan screamed, dropping like a stone to the floor.

Peter dived, then he looked back at the splintered french windows as a tall man with white hair and thick, white, mutton-chop whiskers stepped through them. He was wearing a khaki safari jacket and a large, round

83

pith helmet, and he was carrying an outsize shotgun. The skin of his face was weathered and expressionless. His eyes scanned the room without blinking. This must be the person Alan called Van Pelt.

Peter heard a rustling noise and was amazed to observe Alan scurrying away on his hands and knees, crawling frantically towards the doorway at the other end of the room. Without hesitation, the tall, white-haired man raised his shotgun.

Blam! The noise made Peter's ears ring. Across the room, the blast ripped a gaping hole half-way up the doorpost, showering Alan with splinters. Alan got to his feet and ran.

'This isn't a bloody foot-race, lad!' Van Pelt shouted in a regal British accent. 'Stand up straight and let me pop you fair and square!'

It was clear that Alan had other plans. The great white hunter pursed his lips and stepped through into the living room. Peter and the girls cowered back in terror, but Van Pelt showed no interest in them as he followed Alan's trail.

Blam! They heard another shot in the hallway. Peter bit his lip. Had Alan been killed?

'Blast it!' Van Pelt shouted out in frustration. 'You're a disgrace to the species!'

Peter heard the front door creak loudly. Alan must have escaped! Peter jumped up and set off towards the front hall.

'Where are you going?' Judy shouted.

Peter didn't have time to answer; he had to see what was going to happen next. He got to the doorway just in time to see Alan running into the street. The police car was just pulling up as Alan raced past it. It looked as if the car had suffered a lot of wear and tear since Peter had last seen it. Not only was there a big hole in the roof, but now it was also dented and scratched all over.

A second later, Officer Bentley was jumping out of his car. 'Hey, you!' he shouted at Alan.

Blam! The shotgun went off, disintegrating a branch of the tree just above Alan's head. At the sound of firing, Officer Bentley spun around, crouched behind his police car and drew his revolver.

'Drop that gun!' he shouted at Van Pelt. 'Get your hands in the air!'

Blam! The great white hunter responded by blasting away at the patrol car. Officer Bentley instantly ducked.

Blam! Blam! Blam! In rapid succession Van Pelt blew out the car's windscreen, its rear window, the headlights and, for good measure, the streetlight above Officer Bentley's head, sending a shower of glass down on him.

Meanwhile Alan was still racing down the street. Van Pelt took aim at him. To Peter it looked as if he had a clean shot. Peter shut his eyes, waiting for the blast.

Click! No blast. Peter opened his eyes and saw Van Pelt glance down at his gun with a look of disgust.

'Blast it all!' the great white hunter growled, then he sprinted away through a hedge, as if trying to find a short cut in order to catch Alan. Peter could only assume that he'd run out of ammunition.

For a moment there was quiet everywhere. Then Officer Bentley crawled out from behind the door and inspected the remains of his brand-new patrol car. He then jumped in and drove away at speed, his tyres smoking as he went, squealing, down the street.

Peter looked around and noticed that some of the vine seeds had floated out of the house and were drifting away in the breeze. He felt his shoulders sag. Alan was running for his life. Now they'd never get to finish the game. It was all hopeless.

15

In the depths of depression, Peter, Judy and Sarah trudged back into the house and made for the living room.

'Something tells me that hunter guy has been looking for Alan for a long time,' Judy said as they crossed the hall.

'You're right,' Sarah said. 'And even if Alan gets out of *this* situation, the same thing is going to keep happening to him over and over again.'

Peter gave her a curious look, as if wondering how she could be so sure.

'When you carry so much repressed anger, it attracts a lot of negative energy,' Sarah explained. 'Alan didn't end up in the jungle by accident. There *are* no accidents.'

They entered the living room. The walls were covered in vines and purple flowers.

'Whose turn is it?' a voice asked.

Peter and the girls spun around, startled to see Alan climbing in through the living-room window.

He gave Sarah a wry smile.

'I go next,' Judy said.

Meanwhile Sarah was glowering at Alan. 'You might have warned us that there was someone in there with a gun, trying to kill us.'

'Is that hunter the reason you didn't want to play?' Judy asked Alan innocently.

'He didn't want to play either?' Sarah gasped, pointing an accusing finger at Alan. 'Well, well, well, Mr We-Started-Something-And-Now-We're-Gonna-Finish-It. The truth comes out.'

'Why is he trying to kill you?' Peter asked.

'He's a hunter,' Alan replied simply. 'Right now he happens to be hunting me.'

'But why?' Judy persisted.

'I really don't know,' Alan said with a sad shrug. 'He seems to find everything about me so . . . offensive. You'd think he wouldn't want to waste his time.'

'Have you ever tried sitting down and working out your differences?' Sarah asked.

'Are you *crazy*?' Alan asked. 'You can't talk to him. He's –'

'Don't you *dare* call me crazy!' Sarah screamed, interrupting him. 'Everyone thinks I'm crazy. Ever since I told the cops twenty-six years ago that you had disappeared inside a board game.'

'I wasn't calling you crazy,' Alan said apologetically. 'It was just a figure of speech.'

'Maybe I should roll,' Judy said impatiently, trying to attract their attention. Alan and Sarah simply ignored her.

'You know what it's like to be known as the little girl who saw Alan Parrish murdered?' Sarah asked emotionally. 'You think anyone came to my fourteenth birthday?'

'Not even Billy Jessup?' Alan asked. 'It sounds like his kind of scene.'

'Billy who?' Sarah frowned as if she didn't know who Alan was referring to.

'Oh, come off it, Madam Serena,' Alan scoffed. 'I'm sure if you dig around in the lower reaches of your higher consciousness, you ought to be able to dredge up the memory of your boyfriend, Billy. You were the perfect match. *His* anger wasn't repressed.'

Peter had heard enough of this namecalling. He turned to his sister. 'Go ahead, roll.'

Judy rolled the dice and her token advanced. A new rhyme floated up into the crystal lens: 'Don't be fooled, it isn't thunder. Staying put would be a blunder.'

Peter and his sister exchanged looks of

puzzlement. Meanwhile Alan and Sarah were *still* bickering.

'Are you talking about that kid who used to take your bicycle?' Sarah asked.

'I'm talking about the guy you went to the movies with when you should have been finishing the game we started,' Alan shot back.

Under his feet Peter could feel a gentle vibration coming from the floor. It was like the sensation of a train coming towards them, but still very far away.

Oblivious to everything else, Sarah and Alan continued their argument.

'You were always so immature,' Sarah said. 'You're *still* immature!'

'I'm immature? At least I –' Alan suddenly stopped. 'You hear that?'

Now Peter could hear a distant rumbling sound that went with those vibrations. Alan walked over to the wall and put his hand on it. For a moment they all held their breath and kept perfectly still. The vibrations seemed to be growing stronger and the rumbling was definitely getting louder.

Alan spun around. 'Stampede!'

He rushed towards Peter and the girls, driving them away from the wall.

Crash! Over his shoulder, Peter glimpsed a sight that was more mind-boggling than anything else he'd seen so far! The long, upward-pointing horn of a rhinoceros smashed through the wall ... followed, a split second later, by a huge rhino that came crashing through the wall as though it was made of paper.

'Run!' Alan roared as more rhinos broke through. The air was filled with an unbelievably deafening din of hoofbeats and snorting.

Peter dived behind a sofa, followed by the others, as the stampeding herd of rhinos charged clean through the living room.

Crash! Without a pause, they smashed their way headlong through the west wall of the house and created a huge hole leading out to the lawn!

The thunder of pounding feet and wild trumpeting followed as a herd of rampaging elephants came next, followed by a racket of zebra hoofs.

Moments later, all that remained was a cloud of dust and an eerie silence. The path the animals had taken extended from one end of the living room to the other. Every object – table, lamp or chair – in their path had been pulverized. Peter and the others slowly rose from behind the couch to survey the damage. It looked exactly as if a column of tanks had rumbled through.

Just when it seemed that nothing worse could happen, a flock of pelicans took them by surprise, gliding silently through the hole at the east end of the living room. The birds all passed right through except the last one, a big feathery fellow which landed amidst the rubble near the game board.

The big bird cocked its head, eyeing the board, then without warning snatched it up in its bill and took off!

'Don't let him get away!' Alan cried.

The big bird flew back towards the hole in the east wall, but Alan and Judy stood there, blocking it and waving their arms excitedly. The pelican banked and headed towards the west wall and the open sky beyond.

'Sarah! Peter!' Alan yelled. 'Stop him!'

Peter raced behind Sarah towards the big gaping hole in the wall that led out to the lawn. When they got there, they stood in front of it, waving their arms just as Alan and Judy had done. The pelican made for Sarah first, but at the last moment it veered off course . . . straight towards Peter!

Peter had never seen such a big bird. Its wing-span must have been over six feet! The giant pelican dived, its long, pointed beak aimed directly at Peter's head. Peter stood his ground, waving his arms. The pelican had turned away when the others did that. Why didn't it turn away now? It didn't. It just kept coming and coming . . .

16

At the last second Peter ducked and covered his head with his arms. The pelican swooped past him and out through the hole in the wall; then it flapped away through the trees.

Giving Peter a disgusted and scornful look, Alan sprinted towards the hole.

Peter bit his lip with the humiliation of it. 'I'm sorry,' he tried to say. 'That pelican scared me.'

Alan took no notice of him but raced away in pursuit of the bird.

Sarah came up behind Peter and put her hand reassuringly on his shoulder. 'Don't let him get to you,' she said softly. 'He's the *last* person you want as a role-model.'

Joining them, Judy pointed at the departing Alan. 'Where's he going?'

'Probably towards the water,' Peter guessed. 'That's what pelicans like, isn't it?'

'We'd better follow,' Judy said. But the words were hardly out of her mouth when the muffled sound of a telephone bell reached their ears.

Looking around at the wreckage in the room, it was hard to believe that a telephone had survived without at least being knocked off its hook. Judy followed the ringing sound and found the phone under a mound of broken wood and plaster. Peter stood near by and listened as his sister spoke.

'Hello? ... Oh, hi, Aunt Nora ... Well, I can't really talk right now ... No, a stampede of wild animals just ran through the house. And a dozen monkeys destroyed the kitchen, and there's this huge lion locked in your bedroom. Right ... No, I understand ... OK, bye.'

With a frown, Judy hung up the phone, then she looked at her brother. 'I just got grounded for another week.'

Meanwhile Sarah was gazing through the big hole in the living-room wall. 'This goes against my best instincts, kids,' she said. 'But I think we'd better go see what Alan's up to.'

They made their way out of the hole, then through the woods towards the Brantford River. Soon they were tramping around among the trees and snapping the twigs that lay near the riverbank. Not far away they could hear the churning sound of rushing water.

'Alan?' Judy called out.

'Shhhhhhhhh!' came the reply.

Peter and the others stopped and looked around. Alan was crouching near by, behind some tall reeds, waving excitedly at them to get down. Everyone knelt and watched while he crept through the reeds and bulrushes. Finally he parted the reeds and they could all see the pelican, perched on a big flat rock that stuck out a few feet into the river. The Jumanji game was lying at its feet near the edge of the rock, from where it could fall into the river at any moment.

Peter could see the fix Alan was in: not only did he have to try to get the board away from the pelican, he had to make sure that the game didn't fall into the water. Alan started to worm his way up on to the rock. So far the pelican hadn't seen him.

Then all at once the bird spun around and glared at him!

'Easy there, bud,' Alan said, stretching his hand out towards the game board. 'You've got something of mine.'

The pelican's reply was to jerk its head forward and snap at Alan's hand with its beak.

'Yeow!' Alan pulled his hurt hand back and cradled it. Watching near by, Peter and the girls winced as they imagined Alan's pain.

But Alan would not be deterred. Now he crawled over to another part of the rock that hung out over the water. 'OK, let's try the barter system,' he said.

As Peter and the others watched, amazed, Alan stared down in the water, then suddenly he thrust his hand in and came up with a large, flapping trout!

'Unreal!' Peter gasped.

Alan was on his feet in an instant, dangling the fish in front of the bird, which hopped eagerly towards him.

'Oh, you like this, huh?' Alan tossed the fish on to another part of the rock. The pelican lurched forward and scooped it up with its beak. At the same time, Alan reached for the game board and . . . missed!

Splash! The board fell into the water and started to float downstream with the current.

Peter leapt to his feet and charged out of the bushes and started to run towards the riverbank. Leaping over rocks and fallen trees, he set off downstream, hoping to get ahead of the game board and intercept it.

But now it was being swept out into the middle of the river. He'd never be able to get it!

Just then Peter spotted the fallen trunk of a tree which was jutting out over the water. He hesitated for just a second, then jumped up on to the trunk. He crawled out over the river, but the trunk was too high above the water for him to reach down far enough.

There was only one thing Peter could do. He crawled further out, on to a branch that was about as broad as the thickest part of a baseball bat. Even then he was too high up to reach the water – but if he hung upside down with his legs crossed over the branch, his fingers almost reached the surface.

The Jumanji game was floating quickly towards him in the current. Hanging upside down, Peter started to swing up and down, making the branch creak and bounce. One . . . two . . . three! He bobbed down, grabbed the box, then swung back up!

A second later, he was crawling back along the tree-trunk to the bank with the box safely in one hand. Judy and Sarah were waiting at the base of the tree, watching him with excited and amazed looks on their faces.

'Peter, that was *so* cool!' Judy gushed.

'Very intense,' Sarah added with a smile.

But, much as Peter enjoyed their praise, it was Alan he needed to hear from the most.

'Nice work,' Alan said tersely, then he started to turn away. 'Now let's get a move on.'

Peter felt his shoulders sag in disappointment. Alan didn't seem to be impressed at all.

From where they were at present, the fastest route home lay over an iron bridge that crossed the river. Peter and the girls started across it, with Alan stalking on ahead.

Screech! Officer Bentley's battered and dented police car suddenly came to a skidding halt beside them. Alan started to run, but Officer Bentley jumped out and grabbed him.

'Wouldn't you know an All Points Bulletin to pursue a stampede of wild animals would lead straight to *you*,' Bentley grunted as he twisted Alan's arm behind his back.

'I don't know what you're talking about,' Alan replied.

'Fine.' Officer Bentley started to push him towards the patrol car. 'I'm taking you in for questioning.'

Alan dug his heels in and fought back. 'I'm not going anywhere.'

'Oh, really?' In a flash, Officer Bentley had slapped a pair of handcuffs on Alan and started to *drag* him towards the car.

Peter knew they had to stop him: once Alan was gone, they'd *never* be able to finish the game.

'Wait a minute!' Sarah cried desperately. 'Please ... uh ... don't take him away ... He's ...'

'Her fiancé,' Judy finished the sentence for her.

Officer Bentley stopped in his tracks and frowned. 'I thought you said he was your uncle.'

'He is,' Judy said. 'But he's the half-brother of my mother's sister from her father's first marriage.'

For a moment everyone was con-fused. Then Peter decided to chime in with his own phoney plea: 'Please don't take our half-uncle. He's the only family we've got.'

Something weird must have happened, because all of a sudden Alan changed his mind and started bobbing and jerking around like a crazy person as he tried to drag Officer Bentley towards the car.

'It's all right!' Alan cried. 'I'll be back soon. Let's go, Carl.'

He pulled Officer Bentley towards the patrol car, as if he couldn't wait to be taken down to police headquarters and questioned.

Sarah was outraged. '*You* were the one who said you'd never abandon your friends!' she screamed at him. 'And now you're just leaving us holding the bag.'

'A bag's going to be holding *me* if you don't let me get out of here,' Alan yelled, frantically tugging at the handcuffs. 'Van Pelt's got me in his sights. Carl! Come on!'

Everything was going crazy, and it was all because of the game. Suddenly Peter had a stroke of genius. He knew everything was supposed to go back to normal once the game was finished. So, what if he just finished the game by himself?

With everyone else still yelling at Alan, and with Alan himself hopping around as if he had ants in his pants, no one noticed when Peter wandered off to one side and opened the game board.

His token was exactly twelve squares from the end. Peter took out the dice and carefully positioned them in his fingers so that both showed six. All he had to do was drop them carefully so that they would fall straight down. Then it would look as though he'd rolled a twelve, and everything would go back to normal.

By now Alan and Officer Bentley were in the patrol car, and Officer Bentley was busy telling the rest of them to go home. Peter let the dice fall.

The next thing he knew, he couldn't move. It felt as though some kind of spell had swept over him. Not only that but, instead of going forward, his token went back to the beginning of the game. A cold, tingling terror swept through him.

'Judy!' he cried.

Judy came across to him and saw that the board was open. 'What's wrong? What happened?'

Peter explained that he'd tried to end the game by himself, and now he couldn't move. New words began to float up into the crystal: 'A law of Jumanji having been broken, you will slip back even more than your token.'

'You tried to *cheat*?' Sarah gasped when she joined them.

Once again Peter explained what he'd done. Meanwhile he was feeling the strangest sensation: his whole body was tingling.

'*Peter!*' his sister gasped suddenly. '*Look at your hands!*'

Peter looked down at his hands. His eyes widened and his chest grew so tight, it was impossible to breathe. Thick, dark fur was growing out of the backs of his hands!

17

First and foremost they had to get Alan out of the hands of the police. Sarah said that in order to do that you had to post bail, and in order to do *that* you had to have money. And since none of them had much money, they'd have to go into town to get some.

They managed to hitch a lift to town in the back of a pick-up truck. Clutching the Jumanji game tightly, Peter could still feel that tingling sensation, and Judy and Sarah kept giving him nervous looks. Every time Peter glanced down at his hands, they looked a little hairier. And for some strange reason, it was getting hard to sit comfortably. It occurred to him that he might be turning into a monkey. After all, the board had said he'd be going backwards . . . back to being a primate?

They got into town . . . or what was left of it. Everything was out of control. Parked cars were scattered, helter skelter, on the pavements. People and monkeys were running in and out of shops, as if they were on an insane shopping spree. A man with yellowed skin and with sweat glistening on his face lurched past them, and a motorcycle raced down the street with three chattering monkeys on board.

Sarah led them to a bank cash machine and slid in her card. She pressed half a dozen keys, but a slip of paper came out saying that the machine was temporarily out of service.

'Darn,' Sarah muttered, searching through her wallet and eventually pulling out a leather-covered chequebook. 'Maybe we can bail him out with a cheque.'

'*Ahhhh!*' Judy suddenly let out a scream.

Peter and Sarah spun around and found the hunter, Van Pelt, right behind them. He was carrying some new kind of high-powered rifle with a long scope fixed to it.

'I'll take that.' Van Pelt yanked the Jumanji game out of Peter's furry hands and waved it at them. 'You can tell that coward that if he treasures this toy, he can meet me at . . .'

Van Pelt looked down at the game and his voice trailed off, while a fascinated expression crossed his face: he'd just noticed the picture of the great white hunter on the board, and that it looked *exactly like him*!

'Help!' . . . 'Look out!' . . . 'Run!' Just then a large crowd of panicked townsfolk came racing past them along the pavement. Van Pelt glanced up, just for a moment, to see what was going on. That was all the time Peter needed. He snatched the game out of the hunter's hands and dashed away, into the street.

Screech! A car skidded to a halt, missing Peter by inches. A big, red-faced man pushed open the car door and jumped out, ready to start yelling at Peter.

Ruuuuuuummmmmbbbblllllle! Suddenly the whole street began to quiver and shake. The red-faced man and Peter both looked up – to see a huge stampede of wild animals bearing down on them. The rhinos were in the lead, followed by the elephants, the zebras and the other jungle creatures. The red-faced man turned tail and fled. Without a second thought Peter dived into the car.

The next thing he knew, the animals were stampeding *right over the car*! Peter ducked down as low as he could and looked up in horror as the roof was flattened and the windows shattered, covering him with nuggets of shatter-proof glass. With every passing animal, the roof was being crushed flatter and flatter. Peter ducked down as low as he could get, and he was surrounded by dust, hoofs and flying debris. The roof kept coming closer until Peter was sure he was going to be squashed.

But the stampede passed, and Peter wasn't squashed. He was, however, trapped inside the crushed car. The rough, tanned hands of Van Pelt reached in. Peter thought the hunter wanted to save him but, instead, the hands closed round the Jumanji game.

'Give me that, boy.' Van Pelt pulled the board out of Peter's hands, then he loped off down Main Street.

'Help!' Peter shouted. 'Get me out of here!'

Judy and Sarah reached into the crushed car and managed to pull him out after a great deal of struggling.

'We have to get that game back,' Sarah said, and she set off in pursuit of Van Pelt, who was hurrying along the street and then entered a large discount store called SIR SAVE-A-LOT. People were running in empty-handed and coming out with TVs, videos and other items which Peter felt sure they'd not paid for.

They ran in and looked down the long aisles for a sign of the great white hunter, but all they could see was people dragging things down off the shelves.

'Look!' Judy suddenly gasped. Half-way along one aisle, the Jumanji board was lying on a glass display case. There was no sign of Van Pelt.

'Wait here,' Sarah said, and she hurried towards the display case. As she reached out to pick up the game, a large, weathered hand came out from behind the display case and closed tightly round her wrist. Van Pelt arose from his hiding place.

'I might have known.' Sarah tried to struggle out of his grasp, but he was too strong.

'When Alan hears that I've got you, he'll come,' Van Pelt said with a confident smile. 'And then I'll bag him.'

'Great plan, genius,' Sarah shot back. 'But how is Alan supposed to find out you've got me?'

With his free hand, Van Pelt raised his new rifle.

Blam! Blam! Blam! He fired it into the ceiling. All round the store, people started screaming and running out through the doors. Sarah began to struggle again. Now Van Pelt levelled the rifle at *her*!

'Don't move, woman!' He made his threat loud enough for everyone in the store to hear. 'Or I'll bloody well blow you to chips and snippets!' Then he gestured towards the fleeing people. 'Alan will hear of your predicament soon enough.'

Meanwhile Judy and Peter had sneaked quietly up to the display case. Judy gave a nod to Peter, who was now more monkey than human. Peter jumped up and bit Van Pelt on the knee with his long, sharp monkey teeth. At the same moment Judy popped up with the counter's laser price-reading gun in her hands and flashed it into Van Pelt's eyes.

'*Yaaaaaa!*' The great white hunter let go of Sarah's wrist and howled as the laser gun blinded him temporarily.

Sarah grabbed the game, and the three of them started to run.

Blam! Blam! Blam! A row of large purple Barney dolls on a shelf above Peter burst apart as Van Pelt fired at them. Peter raced towards the exit doors . . .

But Van Pelt got there first. Peter skidded to a halt.

'Where is she, monkey-boy?' Van Pelt bellowed, aiming his rifle straight at him. Peter swallowed and took a step back, but there was no way he could escape now.

18

'Uh, she's over there!' Peter pointed to the right. The moment Van Pelt turned, Peter took off to the left. With the great white hunter blocking the exit doors, he'd have to find another way of getting out.

A few seconds later, he found himself in the Sporting Goods department, creeping down aisles surrounded by baseball mitts, fishing rods and exercise machines.

Blam! Blam! From another part of the store came the report of Van Pelt's rifle as he hunted for Sarah and the Jumanji game. Peter looked around and spotted an aluminium canoe. Near by, in the diving section, were a couple of scuba tanks.

An idea began to form in his head – but to make it work, he'd first have to find some rope and pay a visit to the department selling laundry soap.

Minutes later, he was busy pouring liquid laundry detergent over the floor in the

Sporting Goods department when Judy came rushing past, pushing a shopping trolley with the Jumanji game in it.

'Psst!' Peter hissed at his sister and got her attention. He motioned for her to join him. Judy skidded to a halt and stared uncertainly at him.

'Peter?' Her forehead furrowed.

'Yeah.' Peter knew why she was frowning: he'd changed almost completely into a monkey by now. 'It's me,' he whispered.

Judy nodded. After all, how many talking monkeys were there? 'What?'

Peter quickly told her his plan.

'Are you crazy?' Judy gasped.

'Got a better idea?'

Judy shook her head.

'OK,' Peter said. 'Just go down to the end of the aisle where the exercise machines are. Wait there until Van Pelt comes by and sees you. As soon as he starts down the aisle towards you, hide.'

Judy just looked at him, with a strange expression on her face.

'What's wrong?' Peter asked.

'I can't believe I'm talking to a monkey,' she said.

'I'm not a monkey,' Peter insisted. 'I'm your brother. Now hurry!'

Peter hid behind a large box of basketballs. No sooner had Judy gone than Van Pelt raced up, breathing hard, his face red with rage and frustration. At the far end of the aisle, Judy stepped out and waved to him. 'Yoo-hoo!'

'You're mine now,' Van Pelt muttered with a vicious grin, and he started down the aisle after her.

But he hadn't gone far before his hunting boots and the liquid detergent came into contact, and he started to skid and dance wildly in an effort to stay upright. This was Peter's cue to jump up and begin Stage Two. He pushed the canoe into position. Strapped on its back were several scuba tanks and strapped across the bow was the longest canoe paddle Peter could find. He lined up the canoe, then lifted a hammer high in the air.

Clang! He hit the valves on the scuba tanks as hard as he could, knocking them open.

Phhoooooossssssshhh! The compressed air shot out of the tanks and the canoe rocketed across the slippery floor . . . straight for Van Pelt!

Clunk! Van Pelt tried to dodge out of the way, but the bow of the canoe slid between his legs and the paddle hit his knees.

Thunk! Van Pelt fell, headfirst, into the canoe, which rocketed down the aisle and through a family of mannequins, all dressed for a camping trip. The mannequins fell to pieces and various arms, legs and heads joined Van Pelt for the rest of the trip, which ended when the canoe went through the door of a large tent. The tent bulged, ripped and collapsed around and on top of him.

'Come on, let's go!' Sarah appeared near Peter and Judy and urged them towards the shop exits.

Blam! They were half way there when a final rifle-shot rang out. Peter stopped and turned around to see what Van Pelt had hit.

'Peter, look out!' Judy screamed the warning.

Peter spun back again, but he couldn't see what it was he was supposed to be looking out for. Then everything went dark as he was buried under an avalanche of tyres! Van Pelt had shot off the lock securing a huge rack full of tyres, just above his head!

Trapped under the tyres, Peter could hear Judy and Sarah racing back and starting to pull the tyres off the pile, trying to free him. Then everything went quiet.

'Stop your cringing.' Van Pelt's deep voice

broke the silence. 'It's unsportsmanlike to shoot defenceless women.'

'That is absolutely the sickest thing I have ever heard!' Sarah replied.

Through a crack in the pile of tyres, Peter saw Van Pelt snatch the Jumanji game out of Sarah's hands.

'He will come to me now,' Van Pelt said in a very self-satisfied voice.

CRASH! Hardly were the words out of his mouth when Officer Bentley's police cruiser came flying through one of the shop's front windows with a tremendous, ear-splitting crash. The large glass window simply disappeared, showering the long rows of tills with glass.

Slam! Bang! Boom! Racks of shelves started to collapse, and their contents flew in all directions as the police car ploughed through aisle after aisle . . . heading straight for Peter, Judy, Sarah and Van Pelt!

19

With one last crash, Officer Bentley's patrol car slammed into a floor-to-ceiling display of paint tins and finally came to a stop. The mountain of cans tumbled down over Van Pelt, burying the great white hunter.

Alan jumped out of the police cruiser. Seeing Sarah and Judy, he gasped, 'You're all right! Where's Peter?'

Judy told him. The next thing Peter knew, Alan was pulling away the last of the tyres from on top of him. Then Alan was looking down at him with an expression of total shock on his face. Peter looked down at himself and understood why: he was now one hundred per cent monkey.

Sarah and Judy quickly explained how Peter had tried to cheat in order to end the game, and how the game had punished him by turning him into a monkey.

'Well, we've got the game,' Alan said. 'The

best thing we can do is get back to the house and finish it.'

'Why can't we finish it here?' Sarah asked.

'The mosquitoes,' Alan explained. 'We can't let them get us.'

Clank! Everyone turned to see Officer Bentley dragging himself out of what remained of his police cruiser. His hand was cuffed to the car door, which had fallen off at the last crash.

For a moment Bentley and Alan faced each other. 'Do you want me to help you?' Alan asked.

'No! Never!' Bentley gasped, more in fear than anger. He set off down an aisle, dragging the door behind him.

'Where are you going?' Alan asked.

'The tool department, where else?' Bentley replied.

Alan turned to the others. 'OK, let's go.'

As they walked out of the store, Judy asked why it was that Officer Bentley didn't want Alan's help. Alan told them how, twenty-six years ago, Carl Bentley had worked on the sole-stamping line at Parrish Shoes and how he'd invented the first air-cushioned, leather-sided, high-topped trainer ever. Then Alan recounted how Bentley had shown him the prototype one day and how he, Alan, had accidentally put it down on the sole-stamping conveyor-belt, where it had got caught up in the machine and had wrecked it, and how that had got Bentley sacked by Sam Parrish himself.

'How did he wind up being a policeman?' Judy asked.

'The town was going downhill and a bad element was moving in,' Alan explained. 'They expanded the police force and Carl got a job.'

'And how did he wind up being hand-cuffed to his own police car?' Sarah asked.

Alan explained how he'd talked Officer Bentley into undoing the handcuffs round his wrists, and how Alan had promptly slipped one cuff on Bentley and the other on the patrol car.

'Why?' Judy asked.

'I had to finish the game,' Alan explained. 'I couldn't let Carl get in the way. But then we heard on the police radio that Van Pelt was holding you hostage here, so I got him in the patrol car and drove down here.'

'How did you know to crash through the window and knock the paint cans on Van Pelt?' Judy asked.

'Well, to tell you the truth, I didn't,' Alan answered sheepishly. 'The car had no brakes.'

By now they were in Brantford Street, just a short distance from the Parrish house. The discomfort Peter had been feeling ever since he had started changing into a monkey was now so bad that it was making him whimper and walk in a funny way.

Sarah gave him a sad look, then she turned to Alan. 'Talk to him, Alan.'

Alan slowed down and walked beside him. 'Well, Peter, you cheated and now you're going to have to face the consequences like a man.'

The pain was almost too much for Peter. He stopped in his tracks and let out a cry.

'Come on, chin up,' Alan said, thinking the cause of Peter's unhappiness was that he'd been turned into a monkey. 'Crying never did anybody any good. If you've got a problem, you've got to face it.'

Peter just sobbed – not because he was a monkey, but because being a monkey *hurt*!

Meanwhile Alan looked as if he'd just realized something of major importance. 'You're right! I'm totally insensitive. Twenty-six years buried in the darkest, remotest jungle and I *still* turned out just like my father!'

The next thing Peter knew, Alan had got down on his knees and was hugging him. 'I'm sorry, Peter. Really.'

'It's not that,' Peter managed to whimper.

Alan looked shocked. 'Then what *is* it?'

Peter whispered something in his ear and pointed down at his trousers. At the bottom of one trouser leg the furry tip of a tail was poking out. Peter had finally worked out what was causing all his discomfort.

Alan nodded and went round behind him.

Ripppp! At the sound of Peter's trousers ripping, the girls turned around and scowled. A moment later, Peter felt a surge of immense relief; he was finally out of pain. Alan had ripped a hole in the back of his trousers, so making room for his tail to hang out.

Alan put his hands on Peter's monkey shoulders and gazed at him levelly. 'Now don't worry, Peter. We'll get you turned back into you in no time flat. We're going right back in there, and sitting down. Together we're going to finish this game, no matter what.'

Peter began to feel reassured. He followed the others on to the Parrish property, up the drive to the front door. Alan pushed the door open, but didn't go in. Instead, he and the others stood in the doorway and gasped.

'Oh, no!' Sarah let out a little wail. The inside of the house was filled with vines:

they covered the walls and anything that touched them. The crystal chandelier in the foyer was covered. Through the green leaves, the light created an eerie, dappled effect on the floor.

'Maybe we should play somewhere else,' Sarah said, backing out of the doorway.

Alan shook his head. 'No, I've been dealing with this stuff all my life. It's the stuff *out there* that throws me.'

At his insistence, they all gathered on the marble floor of the hall and knelt round the game board. Alan put the dice in Sarah's hand. For the first time since their 'reunion' she gazed back at him not with animosity but with an electric longing.

'Ahem,' Judy cleared her throat. 'Sarah, if you roll a twelve, you'll win. The game will be over!'

Sarah closed her eyes and rolled the dice. They made . . . 5.

Everyone sighed with disappointment. On the board, Sarah's piece moved and new words floated up in the central crystal: 'Every month at the quarter moon, there is a monsoon in your lagoon.'

Sarah looked up. 'Monsoon? It's a good thing we're inside. Judy, quick! It's your turn.'

Judy was just about to pick up the dice when lightning crackled overhead. They all looked up in amazement.

'Was it my imagination, or did that lightning happen *inside*?' Sarah asked with a defeated groan.

The words were hardly out of her mouth when a thick, dark cloud formed just below the ceiling.

Rain started to fall.

Inside the house.

Lightning flashed and thunder rumbled. The rain turned into a torrent! In no time the floor was submerged under the water, which was up to everyone's ankles. The Jumanji game started to float away, but Alan grabbed it. Now the water was at their knees and still rising amazingly fast.

'What do we do now?' Sarah cried.

20

'Get to higher ground!' Alan shouted.

They fought their way through the waist-deep water towards the staircase that led to the first floor, but when they got there they could see torrents of water cascading down the stairs from above.

'We have to try to get up!' Alan cried. Each time he tried to climb the stairs, however, he was knocked off his feet and swept back down by the rushing water. By now it was up to their chests and Judy and Peter were treading water in order to stay afloat.

Alan stared up at the chandelier in the hall as if an idea was dawning.

'Come on!' He started to swim towards it.

'*Alan!*' Sarah suddenly let out a scream of pure terror. Alan, Peter and Judy turned and saw the scaly green snouts and bulging eyes of two *huge*, twenty-five-foot crocodiles, paddling along the hallway towards them.

'*Swim!*' Alan cried.

Splashing and churning wildly through the water, the four swam towards the chandelier. Meanwhile the lightning continued to crash and thunder boomed throughout the house. Driving rain pelted down on them. Looking over his shoulder, Peter could see the crocodiles in hot pursuit!

Just then the long dining-room table came floating past. Alan pulled himself up on to it then helped the others on. Peter looked back at the water, rising towards the ceiling in the living room. The crocodiles had gone!

Sarah looked over the edge of the table, down into the water. Suddenly the water exploded in her face.

Snap! Huge crocodile jaws clicked shut, just missing her nose.

'*Ahhhhhh!*' Sarah let out a scream to wake the dead as the crocodiles circled the table, looking for a chance to attack.

'Climb!' Alan shouted, lacing his fingers together so that the others could use them as a step up. Clutching the Jumanji game, Judy climbed up into the chandelier, followed by Peter.

But there was no room on the chandelier for Sarah and Alan. Meanwhile the crocodiles were circling the table, eyeing them hungrily and licking their chops.

Suddenly one of the crocs surged up and clambered on to the far end of the table! The end Sarah and Alan were on shot up like a see-saw and crashed into the chandelier.

The next thing Peter knew, he was thrown off the chandelier into the water!

'Help!' he cried, flailing around in the water.

Meanwhile the table was tilting so steeply that Sarah was starting to slide . . . down towards a crocodile's gaping mouth!

Alan grabbed Peter by his tail and yanked him up out of the water.

'Oh no!' Sarah screamed as her feet landed on the tips of the crocodile's top and bottom jaws. The croc opened and closed his mouth, making Sarah's legs open then close like a pair of scissors as she balanced precariously above it.

Splash! Alan dived past her into the water, pulling the crocodile away from her and wrestling with it. Thrashing and writhing, they both disappeared beneath the churning surface. Hearing the commotion, the other crocodile turned and dived as well.

Now it was two huge, vicious, twenty-five-foot crocodiles against one defenceless man.

'*Alan!*' Sarah screamed.

21

Suddenly and for no apparent reason, the water level began to plummet. It was as though someone had pulled the plug in a bathtub. Alan and the crocodiles began to swim against the current that was sucking them away. From the chandelier Peter stretched out his paw as far as he could towards Alan, who managed to grab it. But the current was so strong, it began to drag Peter off the chandelier.

With pleading eyes, Peter reached out to Judy, and she grabbed his hand. Now *she* was starting to get pulled into the water. Sarah took hold of Judy's hand and held on tight while the crocodiles were swept away.

Now Peter could see that the front door was missing. Someone must have opened it, allowing the water to escape.

The last of the water finally drained away, and the table settled on the floor. Alan jumped up on it and helped Judy and Peter to climb down from the chandelier. Then he offered his arms to Sarah. She slid down into them. Their faces were close as they looked into each other's eyes.

'You wrestled an alligator for me,' Sarah said in a voice that was charged with a mixture of awe and appreciation.

Alan blinked, then he stepped back, as if the moment was too much for him. 'Uh, it was a crocodile actually. Alligators don't have that fringe on their hind legs.'

Sarah pursed her lips in disappointment.

'Come on,' Alan said. 'We'd better get upstairs.'

He started up the stairs. Meanwhile Sarah shook her head. Peter gave her a puzzled look.

'Fear of intimacy,' Sarah muttered and set off up the stairs in turn.

They reached the first-floor landing, but there were vines everywhere. One side of the hall was blocked by one of the giant, man-eating pods. On the other side of the hall the lion was still scratching angrily at Aunt Nora's door, trying to get out.

Everyone looked around nervously.

'We'd better head upstairs,' Alan said. 'The attic's safer.'

They climbed up the spiral staircase into

the attic. Alan wiped his hand over the top of an old-fashioned trunk to clear away the dust, then set the game down. The others gathered round him and slumped down on old crates and boxes; they were exhausted. Alan looked around at their faces. No one had the energy even to speak. He picked up the dice as if he was about to roll.

'Uh-oh.' He stopped. 'Did I forget to collect two hundred dollars last time I passed Go?'

Alan laughed at his own joke, but Peter and the others just shook their heads and groaned, utterly unamused.

'OK, OK,' Alan grumbled. 'There's no law that says you can't have a sense of humour.'

He rolled the dice. His token slid forward automatically and new words floated up in the crystal: 'You better watch just where you stand. The floor is quicker than quicksand.'

Plop! The crate Alan was sitting on immediately started to sink into the floor!

Sarah grabbed the dice and Peter snatched up the board. They dived away from their seats into the corners as the floor under Alan became a thick, rippling, wood-grained ooze. It grew and grew until it was a pool of goo, ten feet across, with Alan in the centre!

The others watched in horror while Alan clung frantically to the trunk until . . . *Gulp!* . . . it sank beneath him. No matter how hard he struggled, he couldn't stop the sticky ooze from dragging him down.

'Alan, don't struggle,' Sarah cried.

'Help!' Alan screamed, struggling for all he was worth. The stuff was already up to his chest!

Judy raced away and came back with a music stand. Alan grabbed one end and she held the other, and . . .

It came apart!

'*Heeeellllllllppppp!*' Alan screamed.

Peter spotted an old trombone and raced to get it. He returned and held it out to Alan, who grabbed the slide, and . . .

It came apart!

'Stop giving me things that come apart!' Alan screamed.

Sarah grabbed an old chair. Holding it by one leg, she held it out to Alan, who grabbed its back, and . . .

It came apart!

Alan groaned. By now he had sunk up to his chin! Sarah slid down on her stomach and plunged her arms into the ooze in a futile attempt to reach him.

Peter could see that it was hopeless.

Nothing could prevent Alan from disappearing beneath the floor – and with him went any chance of ever finishing the game!

22

With the situation looking totally hopeless, Judy tried one last gambit. She
picked up the dice and rolled them, hoping
to throw the number that would bring her
token to the end of the game. Instead of
moving forward, however, her token moved
back, as the following words appeared in
the crystal lens: 'There is one thing that you
will learn. Sometimes you must go back a
turn!'

Having seen his sister's token slide backwards, Peter turned woefully towards Alan
and Sarah – just as something miraculous
occurred: the pool of liquid floor turned
solid again! It looked exactly the same as the
old attic floor, except for one thing: Alan and
Sarah were stuck in it!

Alan's head was tilted back so that only
the front part of his face and his two out-
stretched forearms were showing. Sarah was
on her knees with her hands stuck in the

wood. Once again their faces were only inches apart.

Peter and Judy quickly knelt down on either side of Alan's face.

'Thank you, Judy,' Alan said, wincing. 'That was quick thinking. Sarah and I would like to get out of the floor now. I believe it's Peter's turn.'

Peter and Judy hurriedly returned to the board. Meanwhile Alan's and Sarah's faces were again so close that they were almost kissing.

Sarah giggled nervously. 'In my support group, they'd say we were violating each other's personal space,' she said.

'Is that bad?' Alan asked her.

'Oh, yeah, it's a cardinal sin.' Sarah grinned. 'But I'm kind of enjoying it, really.'

'Me, too,' Alan admitted.

Meanwhile Peter had picked up the dice and rolled them. His token slid to a new spot and fresh words appeared: 'Need a hand? Why, you just wait. We'll help you out, we each have eight.'

The sound of hundreds of scuttling feet filled the attic. Then a spider the size of a cat dropped by a thread from a beam in the attic ceiling!

'*AAAAAHHHHHH!*' Judy and Sarah

howled in unison. Peter spun around and gazed into the dark corners of the attic, where glistening red eyes had started to appear and come forward into the light. Giant spiders! Dozens of them!

With her hands still trapped in the attic floor, Sarah was shaking, paralysed with fear. Judy quickly grabbed the top of the music stand and knocked the closest spiders away.

'Peter!' Alan shouted. 'My dad kept an axe in the woodshed! Get it!'

Peter scampered out of the attic and down the stairs, past the creeping vines and locked-up lion. As he raced out of the back door, he heard someone scream; it was a different scream from Sarah's and Judy's, but he didn't have time to think about it. He ran across the back garden to the shed and grasped the door handle.

But it wouldn't open!

Looking up, Peter saw the reason why: the doors were padlocked. He looked around desperately for something to break the door down. There! A rusty axe was leaning against the side of the shed. Peter grabbed it.

Wham! He slammed the axe against the padlock.

Wham! He *had* to get into the shed!

Wham! He had to get the . . .

Peter stopped and looked blankly at what was in his hands – an axe!

Idiot! Peter raced back towards the house, carrying the axe. He went in through the back door and started to climb the stairs. As he reached the first floor, he came face to face with . . . Aunt Nora!

He *knew* he'd heard an unfamiliar scream before. Aunt Nora was staring at him with her mouth hanging open, as if she wanted to scream but couldn't.

'Aunt!' Peter gasped. He was out of breath and scared silly, and his voice sounded like a screech. 'It's me! Peter!'

'*Ahhhhhhhhhhhhh!*' Nora let out a scream that could have shattered glass and stumbled backwards into the linen cupboard. Peter dashed forward and locked the cupboard door. At least there she'd be safe from giant pods, mosquitoes and spiders!

'Can't talk now!' he yelled through the keyhole. 'Explain later!'

Up in the attic, Judy was beating spiders away with the music stand while Sarah and Alan watched helplessly. Then Alan had a sudden idea.

'Sarah!' he shouted. 'It's your turn! All you need is a seven!'

'What am I supposed to do?' Sarah yelled back. 'I can't roll!'

'Wait!' Alan cried. 'Maybe you can!'

Alan bared his teeth at her. All at once Sarah understood!

'Judy!' Alan yelled. 'Bring the game, quick!'

As Peter re-entered the attic, Judy swatted away one last large spider, then she picked up the game. From under it a poisonous purple flower rose up, arching like a cobra, its poison barbs quivering.

'Judy!' Peter cried. 'Look out!'

23

Too late! The vine lunged and some of its barbs struck Judy on the neck.

Wham! Peter swung the axe down, cutting the deadly flower in two.

'Judy, you OK?' Peter gasped.

'I'm fine,' Judy answered, quickly brushing the barbs from her neck. 'Help *them*!' Still carrying the game board, she hurried over to Sarah.

'Give me the dice,' Sarah said. 'In my mouth.'

Judy held out the dice and popped them into Sarah's mouth; Sarah spat them out so that they fell on the board. Her token started to move, and another rhyme appeared in the crystal: 'You're almost there, with much at stake. But now the ground begins to quake.'

Judy let out a scream and jumped back as another spider swung down, right in front of her face. Peter swung the axe, cutting through the spider's thread. The spider hit the floor and scuttled towards him, but Peter knocked it away with the axe.

'Oh no!' Judy let out another scream. Peter wheeled around and found himself facing dozens more spiders . . . more than he could ever hope to fight off.

It all looked quite hopeless!

But at that moment the spiders froze. A split second later, they were scurrying madly towards the far corners of the attic.

'All right!' Peter shouted triumphantly and raised a furry clenched paw in the air.

'Wait a minute,' Alan cautioned. 'Listen!'

Peter stood stock still. For a second there was neither sound nor movement round him. Then the walls began to rattle.

Thunk! Next to him, Judy suddenly collapsed to the floor. Peter bent down. His sister looked pale, and a fine perspiration had broken out on her brow. Peter sat down and gently put her head in his lap.

'Oh no!' he cried in despair.

'What's wrong?' Sarah asked.

'She was stung by one of the purple flowers,' Peter said. 'What's going to happen to her?'

'We've got to end the game,' Alan said. Then to Sarah he added quietly, 'It's her only chance.'

The floor began to shake violently and the unmistakably loud rumble of an earthquake filled the air. Old furniture fell over and stacks of dusty magazines toppled to the floor.

Peter cradled his sister's head in his arms. 'You're going to be OK,' he said softly. 'Does it hurt?'

'No,' she answered with a grimace.

'Liar,' Peter said, but with affection.

Judy moaned. 'I wish Mum and Dad were here.'

Crack! The attic floorboards began to rise and separate. A fissure appeared at one end of the attic. Wood splintered, plastic fell, pipes and wires snapped and sparked! The ground under the house was splitting and the house was being pulled apart!

As the floor divided in two, Sarah was able to pull her hands free. The boards round Alan's face fell away, leaving nothing to hold him up. Suddenly he found himself over a deep, bottomless chasm!

24

'*Alan!*' Sarah dived forward and grabbed his arms. Now she was lying flat on the floor, holding on to him while he hung over the ever-widening chasm!

A foot away, the Jumanji game teetered on the splintered edge of some boards.

'Grab the game!' Alan yelled.

'I won't let you go!' Sarah yelled back.

Alan pulled one hand free and made a grab for the game – but he missed! The game fell through the different floors of the house, landing on a broken floorboard, far below. Below that floorboard was nothing but an empty, dark, bottomless abyss.

Alan had just one chance left. He broke free from Sarah, grabbed a nearby vine and swung like Tarzan through the house. At the end of the first arc, he gracefully switched in mid-air to another vine, swinging down into the chasm and picking up the game before it disappeared for ever!

He swung up out of the chasm and let go, landing in the middle of the living room. Alan was panting for breath and was close to exhaustion. Wiping a cold bead of sweat from his eyes, he set the game on the floor and pulled the dice out of his pocket. This was the moment he'd been waiting twenty-six years for; it was hard to believe it was finally here. He knelt down and picked up the dice.

'I'm going to do it!' he said to himself. 'I'm going to end this game once and for all!' He lifted his hand to throw the dice.

'*Don't move!*' a voice thundered from behind him.

Alan felt a chill run up his spine and he slowly turned and looked over his shoulder at the figure of Van Pelt, who had his rifle trained on him. In fact, the great white hunter wasn't white any more. Ever since his collision with the paint display at the Sir Save-a-Lot Store, he looked more like the great multicoloured hunter.

'Shouldn't you be running?' Van Pelt asked, puzzled by Alan's reaction.

'Not right now,' Alan replied, turning back to the board, which Van Pelt could not see. 'I've got more important things to do.'

Van Pelt kept his rifle trained on the back

of Alan's head. 'Is this some kind of trick?' he asked suspiciously. 'What's that in your hand?'

'Nothing,' Alan replied.

'Nothing?' Van Pelt's eyes narrowed. 'Then drop it.'

'You'd better do what he says,' Sarah said, entering the room from what remained of the broken, first-floor staircase.

Alan let go of the dice. One fell on the game board and showed a 3. The other hit the edge of the board, bounced off, tumbled across the floor and disappeared out of sight into the crevice created by the earthquake!

Alan and Sarah stared after it, wide-eyed. Without the dice, they'd *never* be able to finish the game!

'You call that better things to do?' Van Pelt asked contemptuously. 'Like play with toys? Playtime is over, little boy. You'd better run.'

But Alan shook his head. He was tired of running. He was tired of being in this game. If it wasn't going to end this way, he was willing to try and end it another way.

'But you *have* to run,' Van Pelt said, looking exasperated and confused. 'I'll even *let* you run until I count three. One . . .'

Alan stood in front of him and didn't budge.

'Two,' Van Pelt growled, staring down the barrel at him.

Alan stared back.

'*Three!*' Van Pelt said.

Alan held his ground. Instead of firing, Van Pelt lowered the rifle and nodded.

'At last you have proven yourself,' the great multicoloured hunter admitted.

Alan smiled proudly. But his smile faded as Van Pelt raised the rifle again and aimed at him.

'You are worthy quarry,' Van Pelt said, starting to squeeze the trigger. 'Any last words?'

Alan's eyes darted around until they chanced to look down at the Jumanji board. To his amazement, his token had moved to the finish! He could feel his eyes popping.

'Uh, Jumanji?' Alan swallowed hoarsely.

Blam! Van Pelt fired!

25

'NNNNNNNOOOOOOO!' Sarah screamed and threw herself in front of Alan.

But the bullet never hit her. A strong wind rose up out of nowhere, whipping and whooshing round the walls of the living room. Sensing that the game was ending, Alan and Sarah fell into each other's arms and held tight, their eyes closed.

Van Pelt suddenly started to melt and vanished. The wind grew stronger, swirling round the house like a tornado with Sarah and Alan at its centre. Then the walls exploded, and everything from the world of Jumanji – the vines, the giant mosquitoes, the spiders, monkeys, rhinos, elephants, zebra and everything else – whirled in, tighter and tighter, until . . .

Shhhuuummmppp! They were all sucked back into the centre of the game board.

Everything became quiet.

Alan slowly let go of Sarah and opened his

eyes. Something had changed. He looked into her face and she into his. She looked . . . like the girl he'd known when he was twelve. Was it possible?

Sarah's thirteen-year-old mouth opened in astonishment as she and Alan recoiled from each other in shock. It was 1969 again! They were kids again!

They heard the front door in the hall open. Sam Parrish strode in, his face as red and angry as the last time Alan had seen him. Alan felt a lump in his throat. His father was alive again!

'Dad,' he stammered. 'You're *back*.'

'I forgot my speech notes,' Sam replied stiffly.

Alan dashed across the room and threw his arms round his father. The man froze; he'd never seen such a display of emotion before.

'Dad, Dad!' Alan gasped happily. 'I'm so glad you're back!'

'I've only been gone five minutes,' Sam said, puzzled.

'It seems like a lot longer to me,' Alan replied.

Sam Parrish laughed uncertainly. Feeling his son's arms round him felt so good that he dropped his usual reserve and hugged him back.

'Hey, I thought you weren't ever talking to me again,' Sam said.

'Whatever I said, I'm sorry,' Alan apologized, and *really* meant it.

Sam gazed down at his son for a long silent moment. 'Look, Alan, I was angry. I'm ... I'm sorry, too. And about Cliffside Academy ...'

'Cliffside?' The name sounded vaguely familiar, but at that moment Alan couldn't remember why.

'Right.' His father nodded. 'Why don't we talk it over tomorrow, man to man?'

Having just recently been a thirty-eight-year-old man, Alan didn't want to be reminded. 'How about "father to son"?' he asked.

'Sure.' Sam Parrish backed away and blinked. 'Hey, I've got to get going. I'm the guest of honour.'

He turned away.

'Uh, Dad?' Alan said.

Sam stopped.

'Back in nineteen sixt – er, I mean ... you know *today*, that machine in the factory that broke? It wasn't Carl Bentley's fault. I accidentally put that shoe on the assembly line.'

He and his father exchanged a long look. It seemed to Alan that his father was finally seeing him in a new light.

'I'm glad you told me, son,' Sam said. Then he turned and went out.

Alan turned to Sarah and smiled. His eyes went to the game board, and the smile disappeared. 'Judy and Peter!' he gasped. 'We gotta get up to the attic!'

He spun around, but Sarah held his arms to stop him. 'They're not there, Alan. We're back in 1969 They don't even *exist* yet.'

She held out her hand and opened it, revealing Peter's and Judy's tokens.

Alan looked down at them and nodded sadly. She was right.

'We're back,' Sarah said. 'Everything's the same as it used to be.'

'Except for one thing,' Alan said, turning and making for the kitchen.

'Where are you going?' Sarah asked.

'To get something.' Alan disappeared and, when he came back a moment later, it was with a paper carrier bag. He put the Jumanji game in it and led Sarah outside.

A little while later, they were riding two-up on his new bike. Sarah was holding the carrier bag in her lap. Alan rode as far as the bridge over the Brantford River and then stopped in the middle. Sarah got off and opened the bag. Alan reached in and took out the Jumanji game, which now had two heavy rocks tied to it.

Ker-splash! Alan heaved the game over the wall of the bridge and watched it plunge into the turbulent river below. He and Sarah watched as the parcel disappeared in the churning waves.

Even after the game had disappeared, they stood at the wall, staring down at the river.

'I'm starting to forget what it's like to be a grown-up,' Sarah said.

'Me too,' Alan said. 'That's OK, as long as we don't forget each other.'

'Or Peter and Judy,' Sarah said.

They looked into each other's eyes.

'There's something I've really been wanting to do,' Sarah said. 'I think I'd better do it before I feel *too* much like a kid.'

She stepped close and gave him a long kiss on the lips. When it was over, they smiled at each other and walked back to Alan's bike, holding hands.

26

THE PRESENT

It was a cold winter's day. Chunks of ice
floated down the Brantford River and icicles
hung from the windows of the Parrish Shoe
Company, where the big sign now read:

PARRISH SHOES — FIVE GENERATIONS OF
QUALITY

Alan Parrish, thirty-eight, walked along the
corridor outside the executive offices. The
walls were covered with red-and-green
Christmas decorations, and a Christmas tree
festooned with baubles stood at the end
of the hall. Alan's hair was neatly trimmed,
his tie was tucked in and his shirtsleeves were
rolled up. A shorter man wearing a rumpled
suit and carrying several thick ledgers under
his arm walked by his side. His name was
Marty, and he was the company accountant.

'The retailers are furious that you're plan-
ning to give away all those shoes again this
Christmas,' the smaller man was saying.

'The kids I'm giving these shoes to aren't going to go out and buy ninety-dollar sneakers,' Alan replied with a smile. 'It's not like anyone's going to lose business.'

'Except *us*.' Marty shook his head wearily.

'Look at it like this,' Alan said. 'When these kids grow up and get jobs, they'll remember Parrish Shoes and become loyal customers.'

As they passed another office, Carl Bentley, now forty-six, came out; he was wearing a dark suit and a tie.

'It's an investment in our future,' he said, as if completing Alan's thought. He put his arm round Marty's shoulder and gave Alan a wink that the accountant couldn't see. 'Come on into my office, Marty. Why don't you and I work out the details?'

Marty nodded, knowing he wouldn't be able to win. He followed Carl into the office and shut the door. On the outside of the door were the words:

CARL BENTLEY – PRESIDENT

That night, Alan, dressed in a Santa Claus costume and wearing a long white beard, was standing in the kitchen of the Parrish house, talking to his father on the phone. A few years ago, Sam Parrish and his wife had retired from the shoe business and had moved to Florida.

'The hiking boot line's been doing great,' Alan was saying. 'Yeah, it's been another terrific year.'

All round him the kitchen tables and worktops were laden with platters of food. The kitchen door swung open and Sarah, her face flushed and radiant, her belly heavy and pregnant, waved to him.

'They're here, hon,' she whispered.

Alan nodded. 'Dad, I've gotta run. My marketing director just showed up. Give Mum my love, and we'll see you in a couple of days.'

Alan hung up and made his way into the hall, carrying two shoeboxes, wrapped in gift paper. The room was crowded with people who'd come for the party. A dozen kids ran around, plucking treats from the Christmas tree and chasing one another. Sarah was standing next to a nicely dressed man in his mid-thirties, and his pretty wife.

'Jim, glad you could make it!' Alan gave the man's hand a vigorous shake.

'Thanks,' Jim Shepherd said. 'This is my wife, Martha.'

Alan said hello. Meanwhile, Jim was

looking around at the crowd. 'Where are the kids?' he asked his wife.

A twelve-year-old girl and an eight-year-old boy were pushing their way through the crowd. Alan felt a moment of shock and had to force himself to recover.

'Here are your kids,' he said.

'How did you know?' Martha looked puzzled.

'Just a guess,' Sarah replied, giving Alan a wink.

'Well, you're right,' Jim said. 'This is Judy and Peter. Kids, meet Mr and Mrs Parrish.'

'Hi.' Peter shook Alan's hand.

'Nice to meet you,' said Judy. Neither showed any sign of having recognized Alan or Sarah.

'We feel like we already know you,' Sarah said.

'Because we've heard so much about you,' Alan added hastily. He gave the shoeboxes to Peter and Judy. 'Merry Christmas, kids.'

The children started to unwrap the boxes. Alan and Sarah watched, utterly absorbed in happiness at seeing them again. Then Alan snapped out of it.

'So, when can you start work?' he asked Jim.

'Well, actually, Martha and I were thinking

about taking a little skiing trip up in the Canadian Rockies,' Jim said. 'Sort of a second honeymoon –'

'*No!*' Alan and Sarah both interrupted him at the same time. The outburst was so unexpected that for a moment the entire room went silent.

Alan looked around at the startled faces and felt his own face grow flushed and red. He turned back to Jim. 'Uh, sorry, it's just that we –'

'Really need to get the campaign for the new line going.' Sarah finished the sentence for him.

Jim glanced at his wife and nodded. 'No problem. We can always take the trip another time. Maybe we'll wait until the summer, and go to the Cape instead. In the meantime, I can start next week.'

Alan breathed a sigh of relief. By now, Peter and Judy had torn open the boxes, and each pulled out a brand-new pair of trainers.

'Cool shoes!' Peter gasped.

Judy read the name on them. 'Jumanjis!'

'What do you think?' Alan asked.

'Great sneakers, weird name,' Peter said with a shrug.

Alan and Sarah just looked at each other and smiled.